NANCY DREW
DREW
girl detective ®

PAPERCUTZ™

NANCY DREW
girl detective®

Graphic Novels
Available from Papercutz

#1 The Demon of River Heights
#2 Writ In Stone
#3 The Haunted Dollhouse
#4 The Girl Who Wasn't There
(coming February 2006)

$7.95 each in paperback
$12.95 each in hardcover

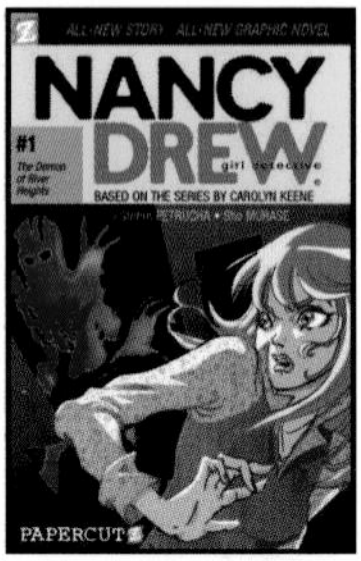
NANCY
DREW
#1
girl detective
BASED ON THE SERIES BY CAROLYN KEENE
PAPERCUT

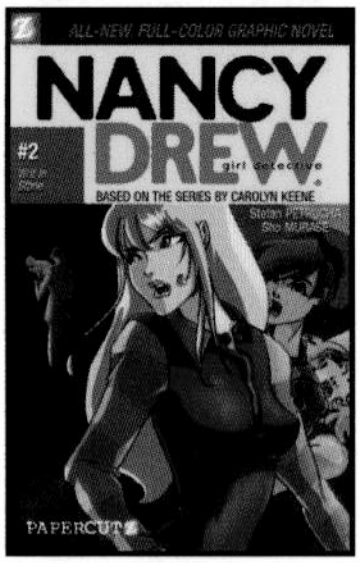
NANCY
DREW
#2
girl detective
BASED ON THE SERIES BY CAROLYN KEENE
PAPERCUT

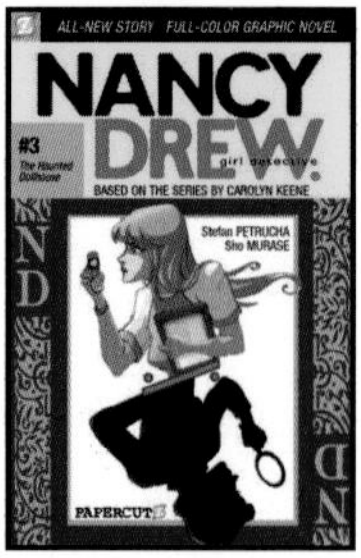
ALL-NEW STORY FULL-COLOR GRAPHIC NOVEL
NANCY
DREW
#3
girl detective
BASED ON THE SERIES BY CAROLYN KEENE
Stefan PETRUCHA
Sho MURASE
PAPERCUT

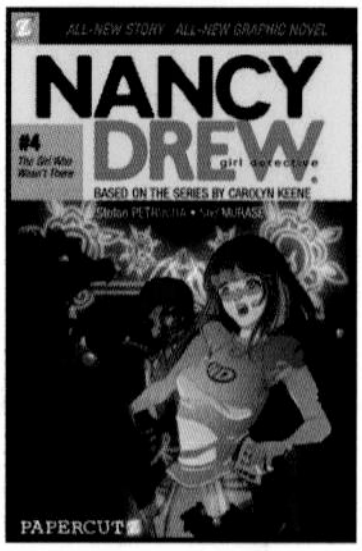
NANCY
DREW
#4
girl detective
BASED ON THE SERIES BY CAROLYN KEENE
PAPERCUT

Please add $3.00 for postage and handling for the first book, add $1.00 for each additional book.

Send for our catalog:
Papercutz
555 Eighth Avenue, Suite 1202
New York, NY 10018
www.papercutz.com

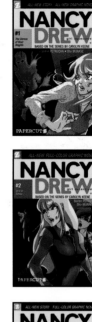

NANCY DREW
girl detective
#3

®

The Old Fashioned Mystery of the Haunted Dollhouse

STEFAN PETRUCHA • Writer
SHO MURASE • Artist
with 3D CG elements by RACHEL ITO
Based on the series by
CAROLYN KEENE

New York

The Haunted Dollhouse
STEFAN PETRUCHA – Writer
SHO MURASE – Artist
with 3D CG elements by RACHEL ITO
BRYAN SENKA – Letterer
CARLOS JOSE GUZMAN
SHO MURASE
Colorists
JIM SALICRUP
Editor-in-Chief

ISBN 10: 1-59707-008-4 paperback edition
ISBN 13: 978-1-59707-008-9 paperback edition
ISBN 10: 1-59707-009-2 hardcover edition
ISBN 13: 978-1-59707-009-6 hardcover edition

Printed in China.

10 9 8 7 6 5 4 3 2 1

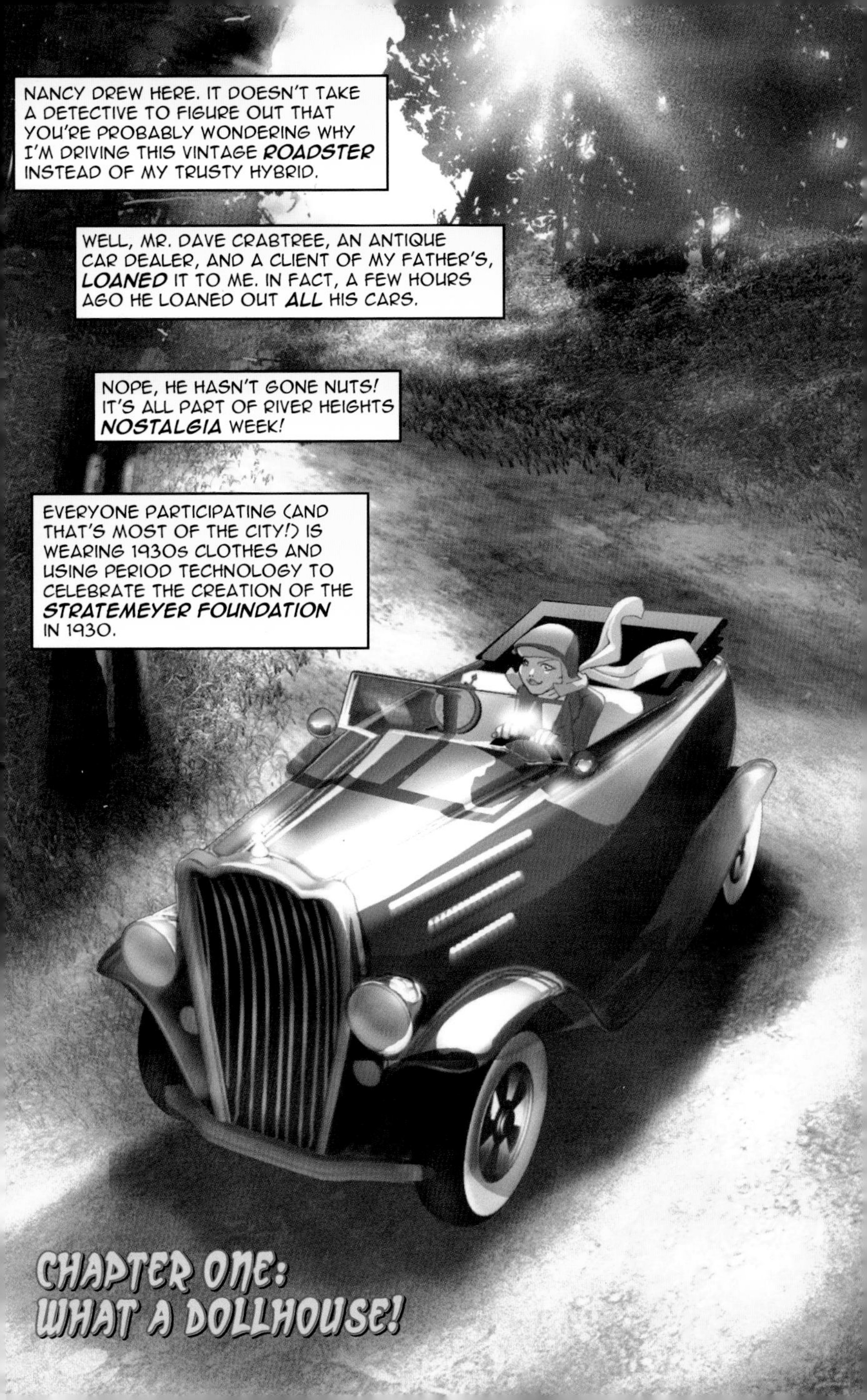
NANCY DREW HERE. IT DOESN'T TAKE A DETECTIVE TO FIGURE OUT THAT YOU'RE PROBABLY WONDERING WHY I'M DRIVING THIS VINTAGE ROADSTER INSTEAD OF MY TRUSTY HYBRID.
WELL, MR. DAVE CRABTREE, AN ANTIQUE CAR DEALER, AND A CLIENT OF MY FATHER'S, LOANED IT TO ME. IN FACT, A FEW HOURS AGO HE LOANED OUT ALL HIS CARS.
NOPE, HE HASN'T GONE NUTS! IT'S ALL PART OF RIVER HEIGHTS NOSTALGIA WEEK!
EVERYONE PARTICIPATING (AND THAT'S MOST OF THE CITY!) IS WEARING 1930s CLOTHES AND USING PERIOD TECHNOLOGY TO CELEBRATE THE CREATION OF THE STRATEMEYER FOUNDATION IN 1930.
CHAPTER ONE:
WHAT A DOLLHOUSE!

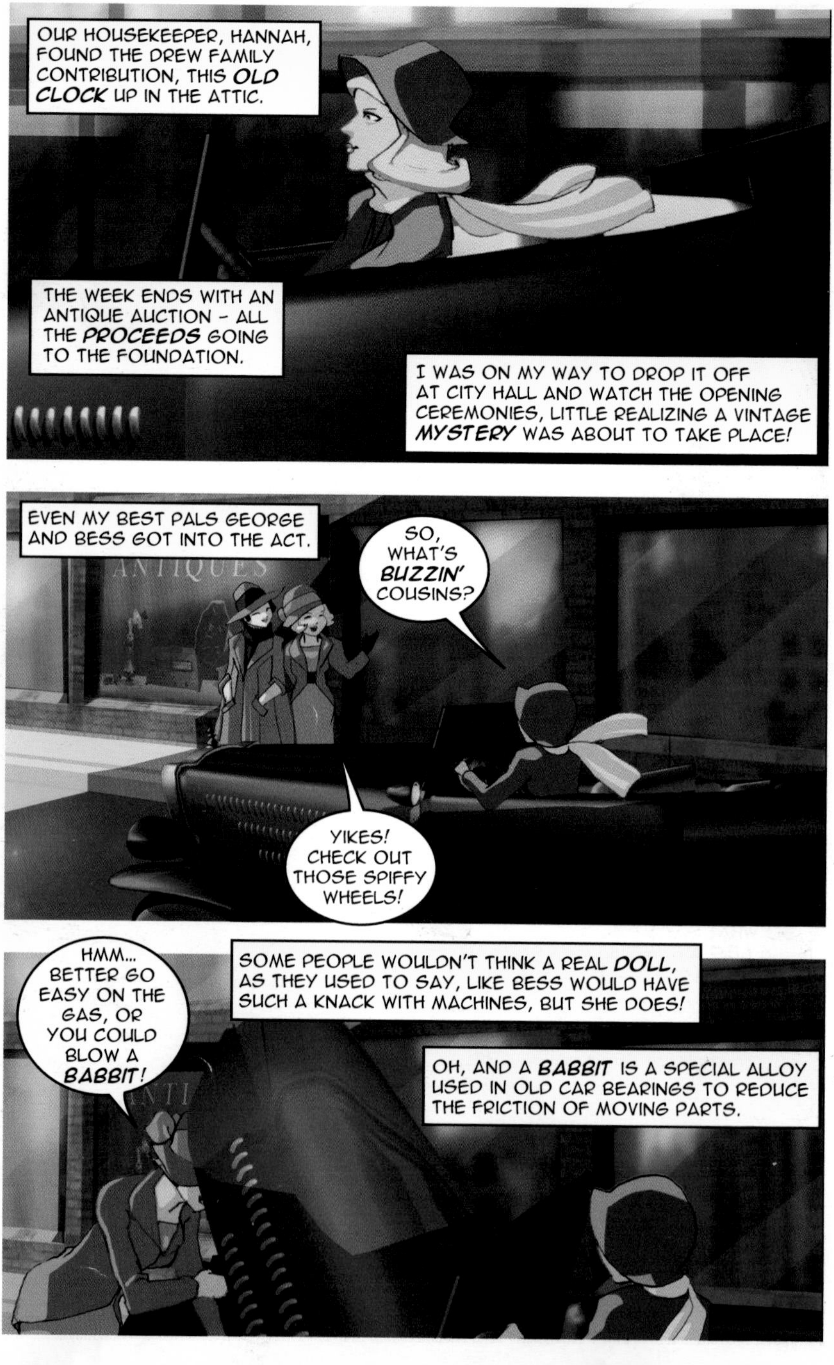
OUR HOUSEKEEPER, HANNAH, FOUND THE DREW FAMILY CONTRIBUTION, THIS OLD CLOCK UP IN THE ATTIC.
THE WEEK ENDS WITH AN ANTIQUE AUCTION – ALL THE PROCEEDS GOING TO THE FOUNDATION.
I WAS ON MY WAY TO DROP IT OFF AT CITY HALL AND WATCH THE OPENING CEREMONIES, LITTLE REALIZING A VINTAGE MYSTERY WAS ABOUT TO TAKE PLACE!
EVEN MY BEST PALS GEORGE AND BESS GOT INTO THE ACT.
ANTIQUES
SO, WHAT'S BUZZIN' COUSINS?
YIKES! CHECK OUT THOSE SPIFFY WHEELS!
HMM... BETTER GO EASY ON THE GAS, OR YOU COULD BLOW A BABBIT!
SOME PEOPLE WOULDN'T THINK A REAL DOLL, AS THEY USED TO SAY, LIKE BESS WOULD HAVE SUCH A KNACK WITH MACHINES, BUT SHE DOES!
OH, AND A BABBIT IS A SPECIAL ALLOY USED IN OLD CAR BEARINGS TO REDUCE THE FRICTION OF MOVING PARTS.

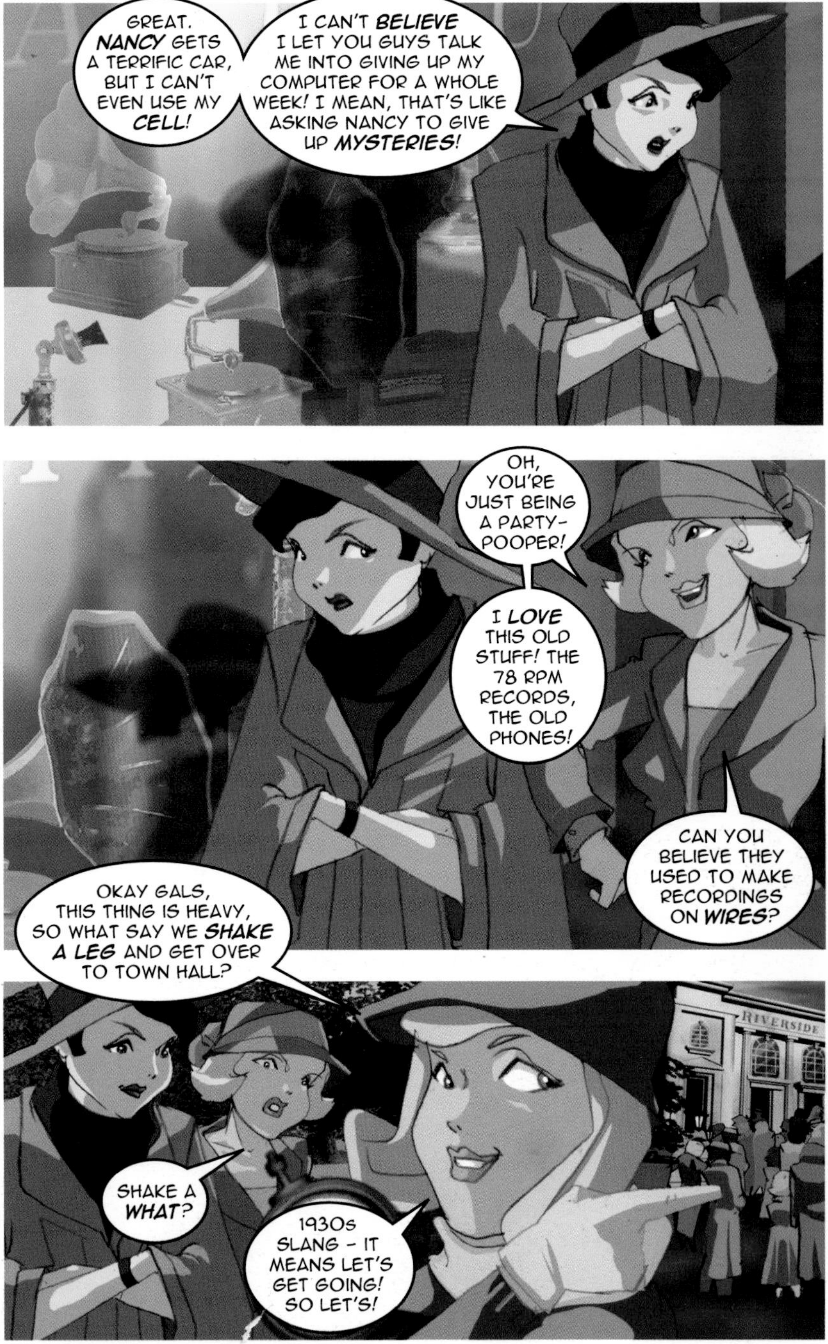
GREAT. NANCY GETS A TERRIFIC CAR, BUT I CAN'T EVEN USE MY CELL!
I CAN'T BELIEVE I LET YOU GUYS TALK ME INTO GIVING UP MY COMPUTER FOR A WHOLE WEEK! I MEAN, THAT'S LIKE ASKING NANCY TO GIVE UP MYSTERIES!
OH, YOU'RE JUST BEING A PARTY-POOPER!
I LOVE THIS OLD STUFF! THE 78 RPM RECORDS, THE OLD PHONES!
CAN YOU BELIEVE THEY USED TO MAKE RECORDINGS ON WIRES?
OKAY GALS, THIS THING IS HEAVY, SO WHAT SAY WE SHAKE A LEG AND GET OVER TO TOWN HALL?
RIVERSIDE
SHAKE A WHAT?
1930s SLANG – IT MEANS LET'S GET GOING! SO LET'S!

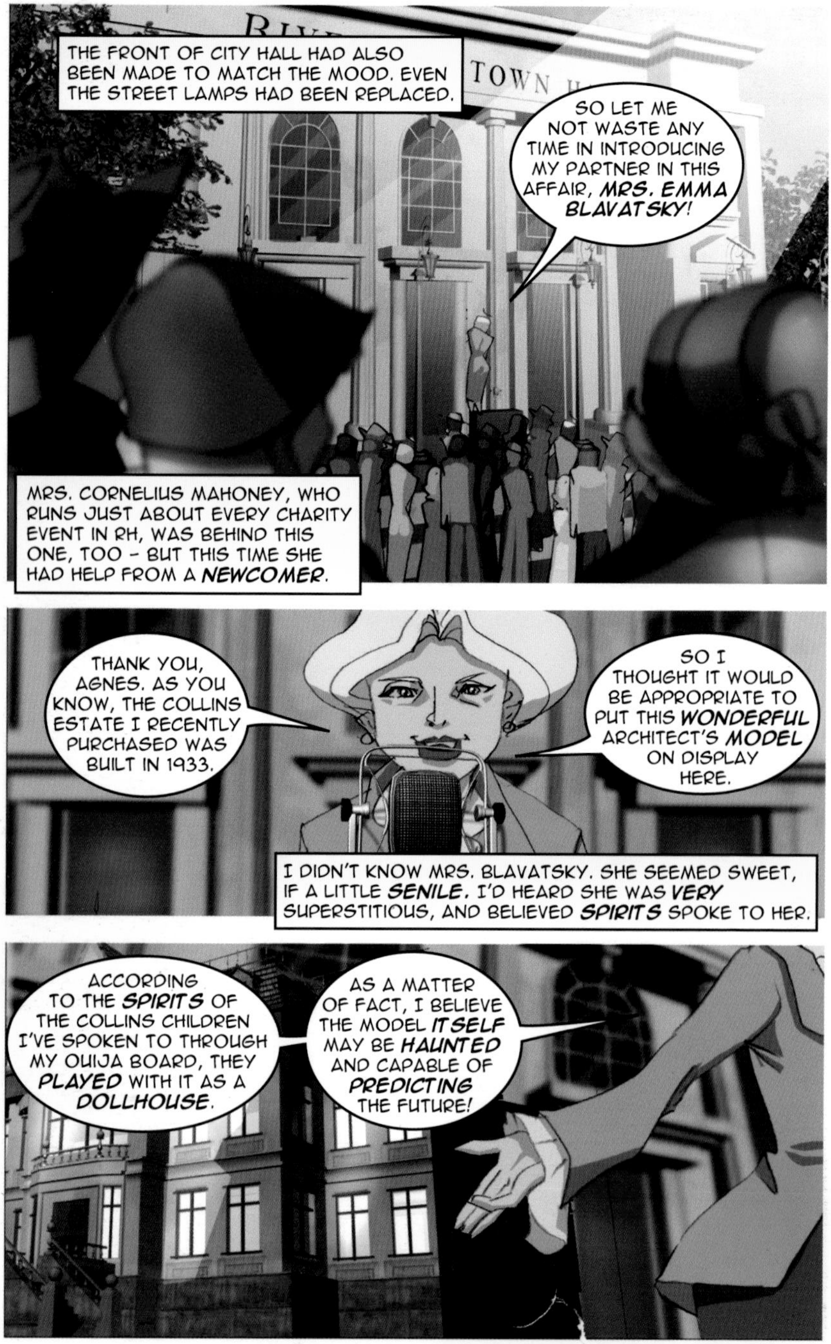

THE FRONT OF CITY HALL HAD ALSO BEEN MADE TO MATCH THE MOOD. EVEN THE STREET LAMPS HAD BEEN REPLACED.
TOWN
SO LET ME NOT WASTE ANY TIME IN INTRODUCING MY PARTNER IN THIS AFFAIR, MRS. EMMA BLAVATSKY!
MRS. CORNELIUS MAHONEY, WHO RUNS JUST ABOUT EVERY CHARITY EVENT IN RH, WAS BEHIND THIS ONE, TOO - BUT THIS TIME SHE HAD HELP FROM A NEWCOMER.
THANK YOU, AGNES. AS YOU KNOW, THE COLLINS ESTATE I RECENTLY PURCHASED WAS BUILT IN 1933.
SO I THOUGHT IT WOULD BE APPROPRIATE TO PUT THIS WONDERFUL ARCHITECT'S MODEL ON DISPLAY HERE.
I DIDN'T KNOW MRS. BLAVATSKY. SHE SEEMED SWEET, IF A LITTLE SENILE. I'D HEARD SHE WAS VERY SUPERSTITIOUS, AND BELIEVED SPIRITS SPOKE TO HER.
ACCORDING TO THE SPIRITS OF THE COLLINS CHILDREN I'VE SPOKEN TO THROUGH MY OUIJA BOARD, THEY PLAYED WITH IT AS A DOLLHOUSE.
AS A MATTER OF FACT, I BELIEVE THE MODEL ITSELF MAY BE HAUNTED AND CAPABLE OF PREDICTING THE FUTURE!

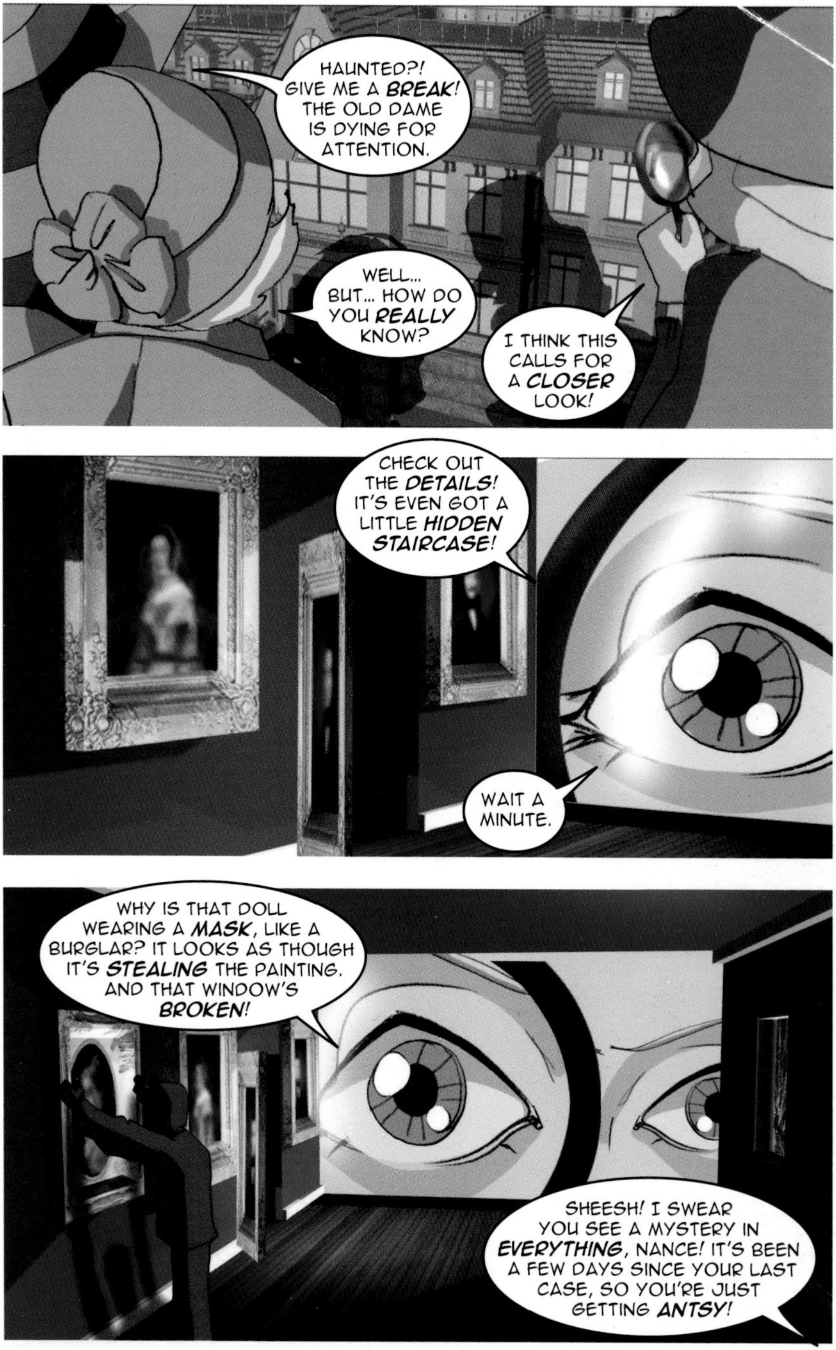
HAUNTED?! GIVE ME A BREAK! THE OLD DAME IS DYING FOR ATTENTION.
WELL... BUT... HOW DO YOU REALLY KNOW?
I THINK THIS CALLS FOR A CLOSER LOOK!
CHECK OUT THE DETAILS! IT'S EVEN GOT A LITTLE HIDDEN STAIRCASE!
WAIT A MINUTE.
WHY IS THAT DOLL WEARING A MASK, LIKE A BURGLAR? IT LOOKS AS THOUGH IT'S STEALING THE PAINTING. AND THAT WINDOW'S BROKEN!
SHEESH! I SWEAR YOU SEE A MYSTERY IN EVERYTHING, NANCE! IT'S BEEN A FEW DAYS SINCE YOUR LAST CASE, SO YOU'RE JUST GETTING ANTSY!

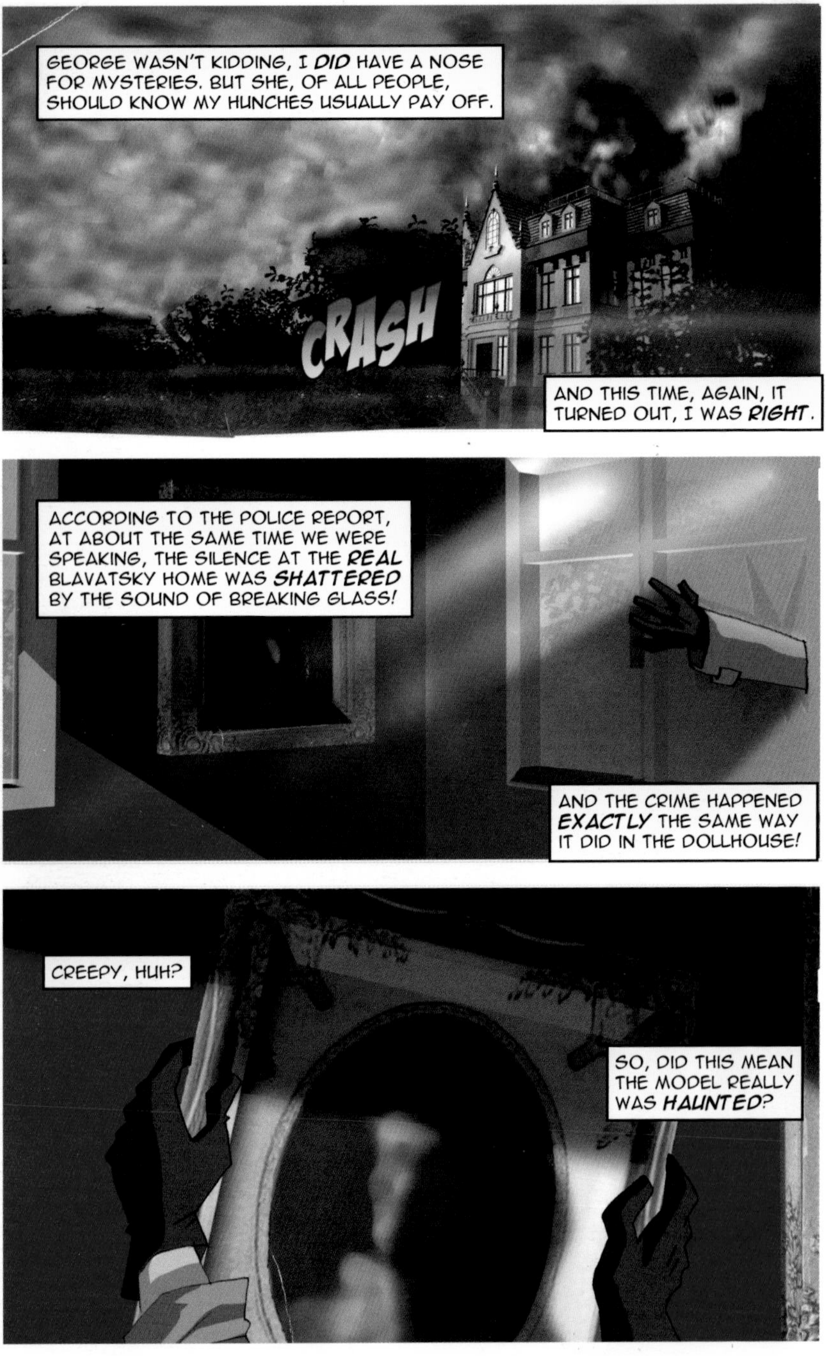
GEORGE WASN'T KIDDING, I *DID* HAVE A NOSE FOR MYSTERIES. BUT SHE, OF ALL PEOPLE, SHOULD KNOW MY HUNCHES USUALLY PAY OFF.
CRASH
AND THIS TIME, AGAIN, IT TURNED OUT, I WAS *RIGHT*.
ACCORDING TO THE POLICE REPORT, AT ABOUT THE SAME TIME WE WERE SPEAKING, THE SILENCE AT THE *REAL* BLAVATSKY HOME WAS *SHATTERED* BY THE SOUND OF BREAKING GLASS!
AND THE CRIME HAPPENED *EXACTLY* THE SAME WAY IT DID IN THE DOLLHOUSE!
CREEPY, HUH?
SO, DID THIS MEAN THE MODEL REALLY WAS *HAUNTED*?

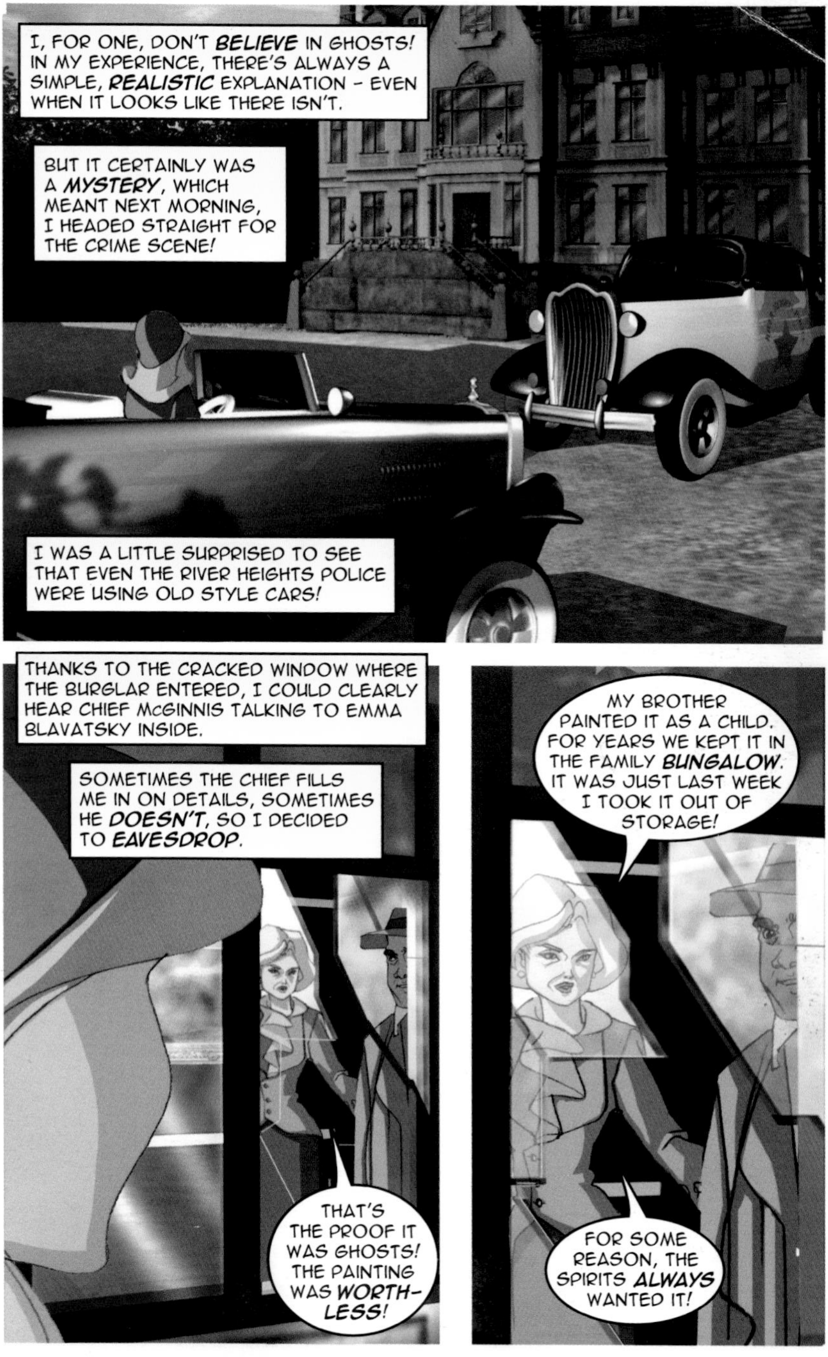
I, FOR ONE, DON'T BELIEVE IN GHOSTS! IN MY EXPERIENCE, THERE'S ALWAYS A SIMPLE, REALISTIC EXPLANATION - EVEN WHEN IT LOOKS LIKE THERE ISN'T.
BUT IT CERTAINLY WAS A MYSTERY, WHICH MEANT NEXT MORNING, I HEADED STRAIGHT FOR THE CRIME SCENE!
I WAS A LITTLE SURPRISED TO SEE THAT EVEN THE RIVER HEIGHTS POLICE WERE USING OLD STYLE CARS!
THANKS TO THE CRACKED WINDOW WHERE THE BURGLAR ENTERED, I COULD CLEARLY HEAR CHIEF McGINNIS TALKING TO EMMA BLAVATSKY INSIDE.
SOMETIMES THE CHIEF FILLS ME IN ON DETAILS, SOMETIMES HE DOESN'T, SO I DECIDED TO EAVESDROP.
THAT'S THE PROOF IT WAS GHOSTS! THE PAINTING WAS WORTH-LESS!
MY BROTHER PAINTED IT AS A CHILD. FOR YEARS WE KEPT IT IN THE FAMILY BUNGALOW. IT WAS JUST LAST WEEK I TOOK IT OUT OF STORAGE!
FOR SOME REASON, THE SPIRITS ALWAYS WANTED IT!

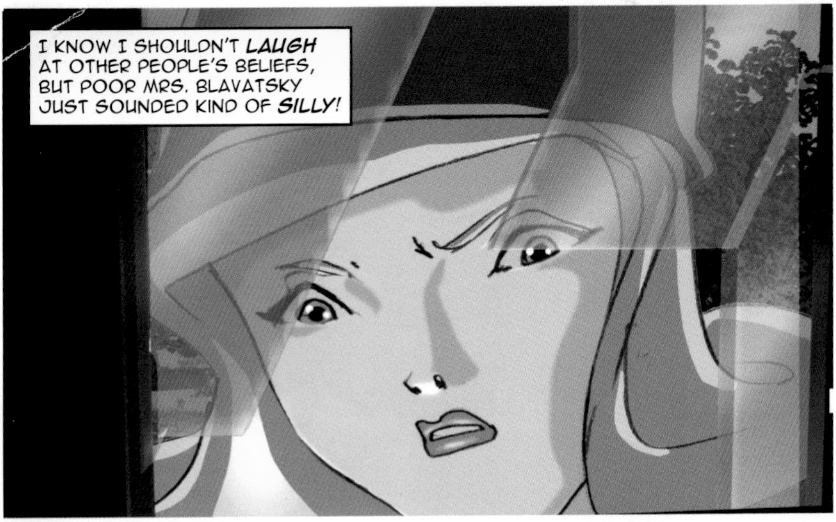
I KNOW I SHOULDN'T LAUGH AT OTHER PEOPLE'S BELIEFS, BUT POOR MRS. BLAVATSKY JUST SOUNDED KIND OF SILLY!

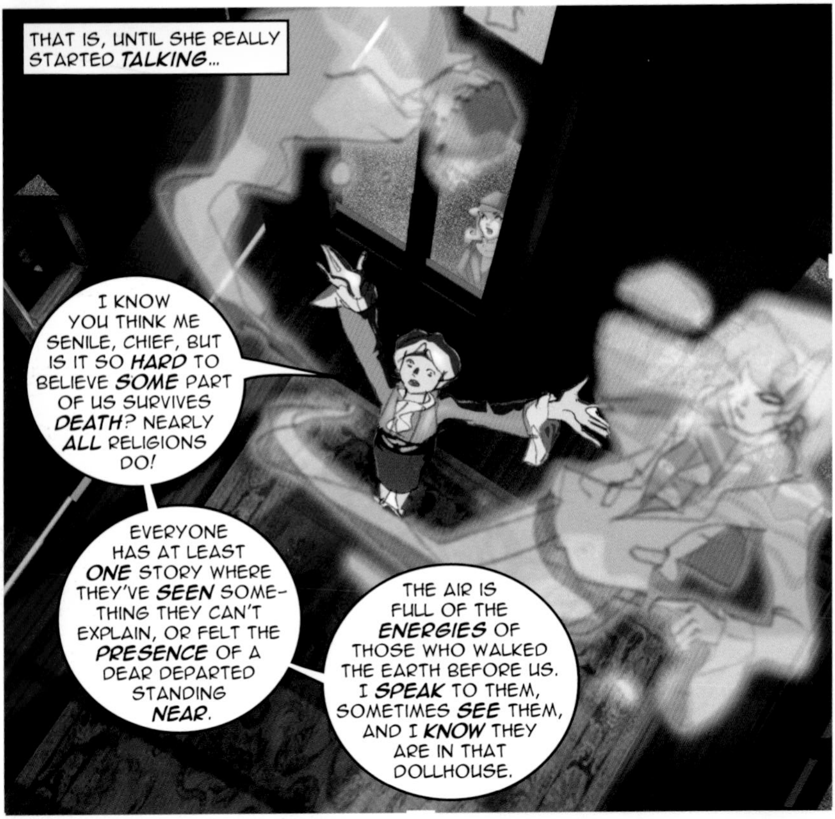
THAT IS, UNTIL SHE REALLY STARTED TALKING...
I KNOW YOU THINK ME SENILE, CHIEF, BUT IS IT SO HARD TO BELIEVE SOME PART OF US SURVIVES DEATH? NEARLY ALL RELIGIONS DO!
EVERYONE HAS AT LEAST ONE STORY WHERE THEY'VE SEEN SOME-THING THEY CAN'T EXPLAIN, OR FELT THE PRESENCE OF A DEAR DEPARTED STANDING NEAR.
THE AIR IS FULL OF THE ENERGIES OF THOSE WHO WALKED THE EARTH BEFORE US. I SPEAK TO THEM, SOMETIMES SEE THEM, AND I KNOW THEY ARE IN THAT DOLLHOUSE.

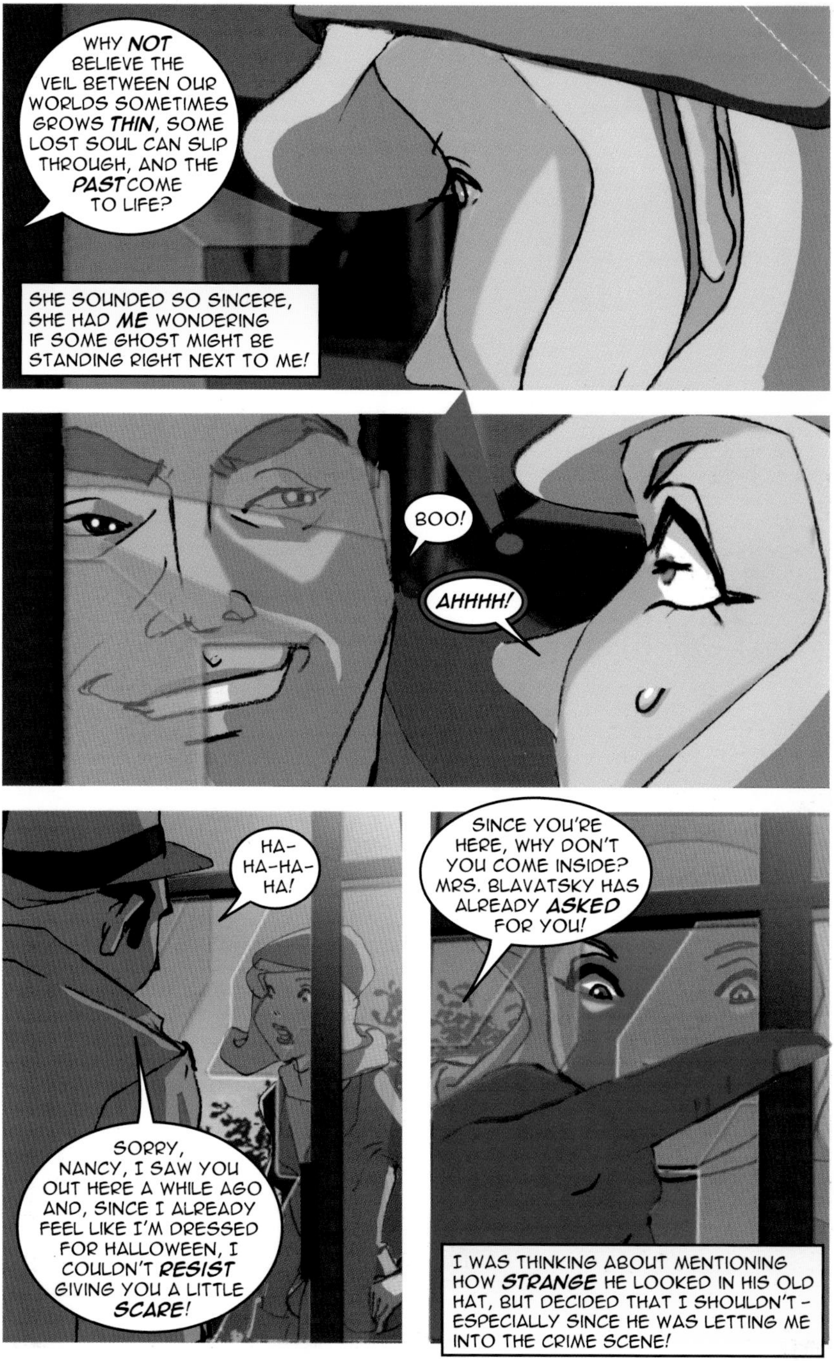
WHY NOT BELIEVE THE VEIL BETWEEN OUR WORLDS SOMETIMES GROWS THIN, SOME LOST SOUL CAN SLIP THROUGH, AND THE PAST COME TO LIFE?
SHE SOUNDED SO SINCERE, SHE HAD ME WONDERING IF SOME GHOST MIGHT BE STANDING RIGHT NEXT TO ME!
BOO!
AHHHH!
HA-HA-HA-HA!
SORRY, NANCY, I SAW YOU OUT HERE A WHILE AGO AND, SINCE I ALREADY FEEL LIKE I'M DRESSED FOR HALLOWEEN, I COULDN'T RESIST GIVING YOU A LITTLE SCARE!
SINCE YOU'RE HERE, WHY DON'T YOU COME INSIDE? MRS. BLAVATSKY HAS ALREADY ASKED FOR YOU!
I WAS THINKING ABOUT MENTIONING HOW STRANGE HE LOOKED IN HIS OLD HAT, BUT DECIDED THAT I SHOULDN'T - ESPECIALLY SINCE HE WAS LETTING ME INTO THE CRIME SCENE!

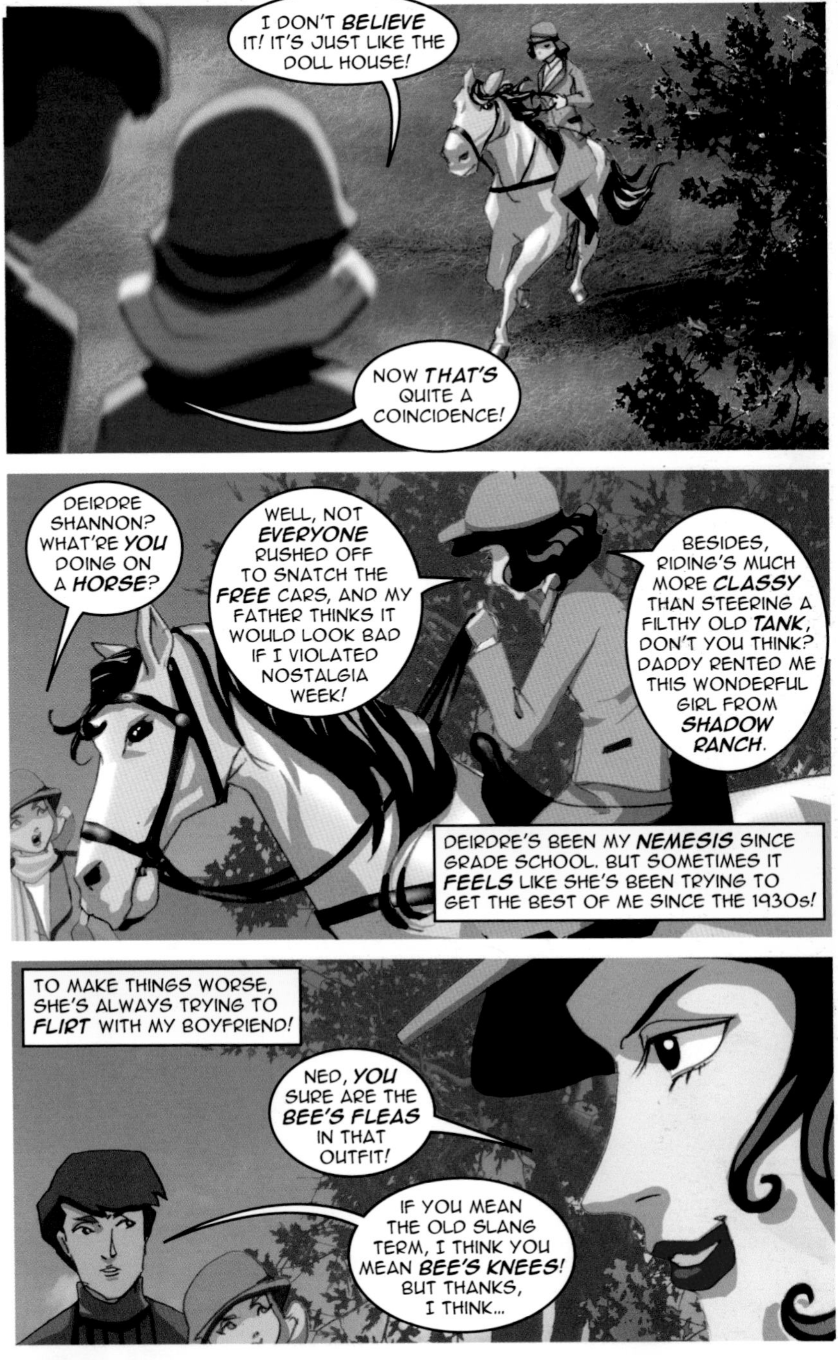
I DON'T BELIEVE IT! IT'S JUST LIKE THE DOLL HOUSE!
NOW THAT'S QUITE A COINCIDENCE!
DEIRDRE SHANNON? WHAT'RE YOU DOING ON A HORSE?
WELL, NOT EVERYONE RUSHED OFF TO SNATCH THE FREE CARS, AND MY FATHER THINKS IT WOULD LOOK BAD IF I VIOLATED NOSTALGIA WEEK!
BESIDES, RIDING'S MUCH MORE CLASSY THAN STEERING A FILTHY OLD TANK, DON'T YOU THINK? DADDY RENTED ME THIS WONDERFUL GIRL FROM SHADOW RANCH.
DEIRDRE'S BEEN MY NEMESIS SINCE GRADE SCHOOL. BUT SOMETIMES IT FEELS LIKE SHE'S BEEN TRYING TO GET THE BEST OF ME SINCE THE 1930s!
TO MAKE THINGS WORSE, SHE'S ALWAYS TRYING TO FLIRT WITH MY BOYFRIEND!
NED, YOU SURE ARE THE BEE'S FLEAS IN THAT OUTFIT!
IF YOU MEAN THE OLD SLANG TERM, I THINK YOU MEAN BEE'S KNEES! BUT THANKS, I THINK...

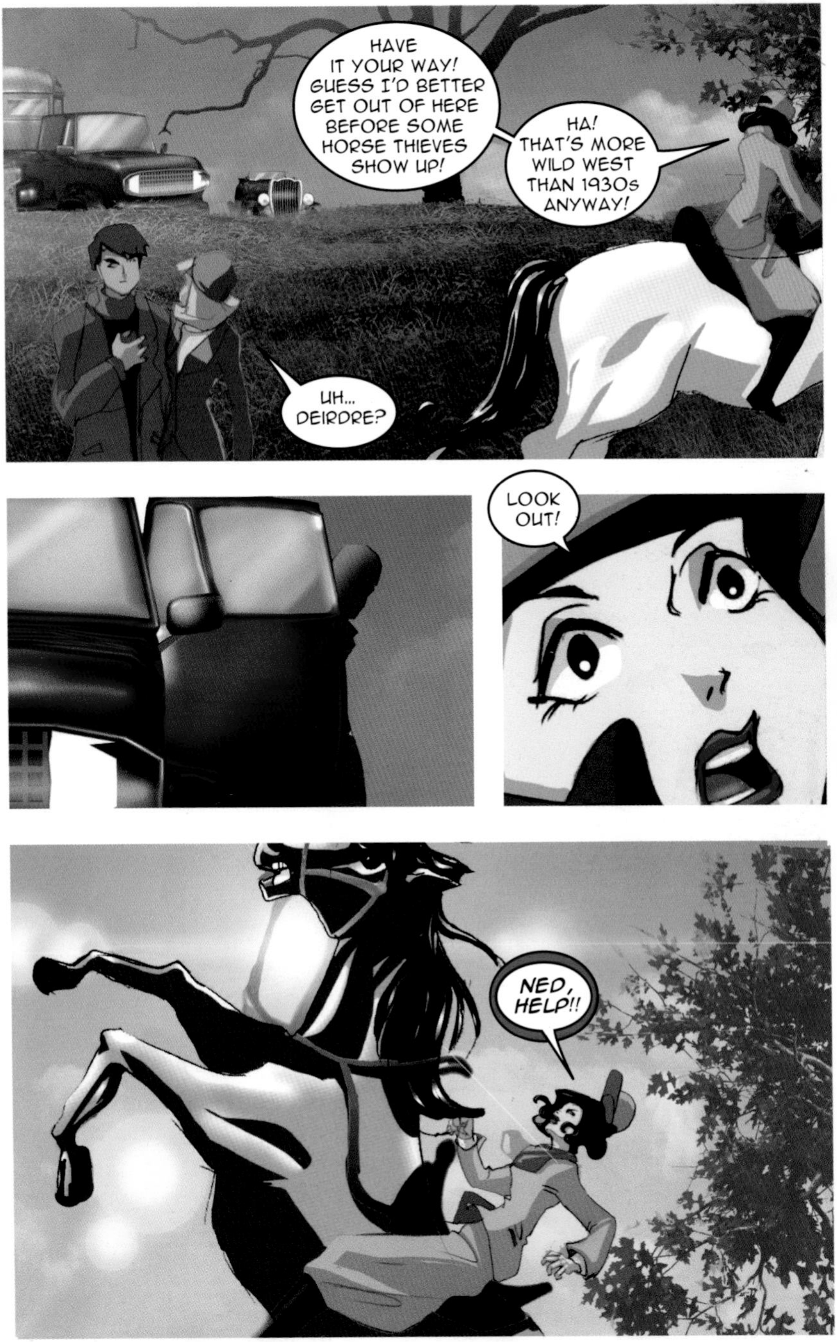
HAVE IT YOUR WAY! GUESS I'D BETTER GET OUT OF HERE BEFORE SOME HORSE THIEVES SHOW UP!
HA! THAT'S MORE WILD WEST THAN 1930s ANYWAY!
UH... DEIRDRE?
LOOK OUT!
NED, HELP!!

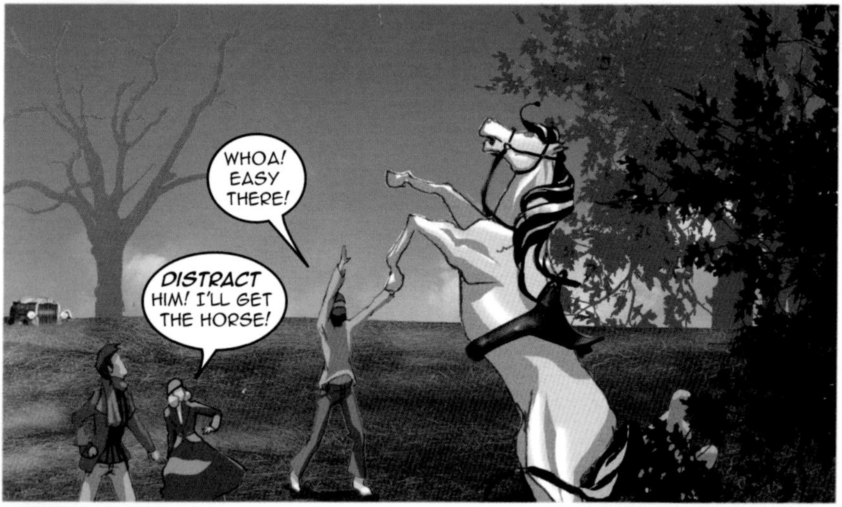
WHOA! EASY THERE!
DISTRACT HIM! I'LL GET THE HORSE!

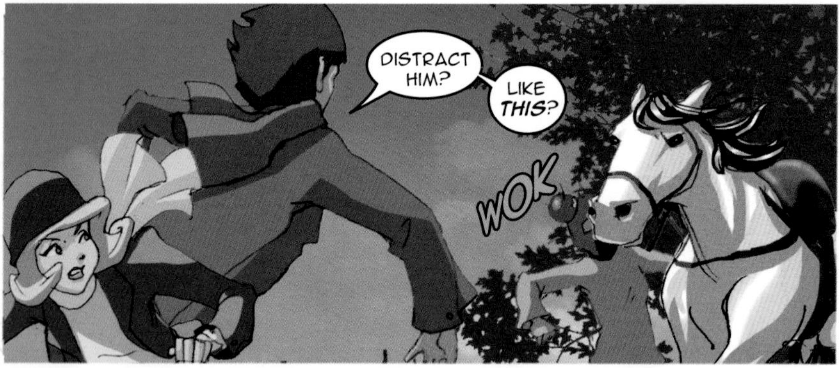
DISTRACT HIM?
LIKE THIS?
WOK

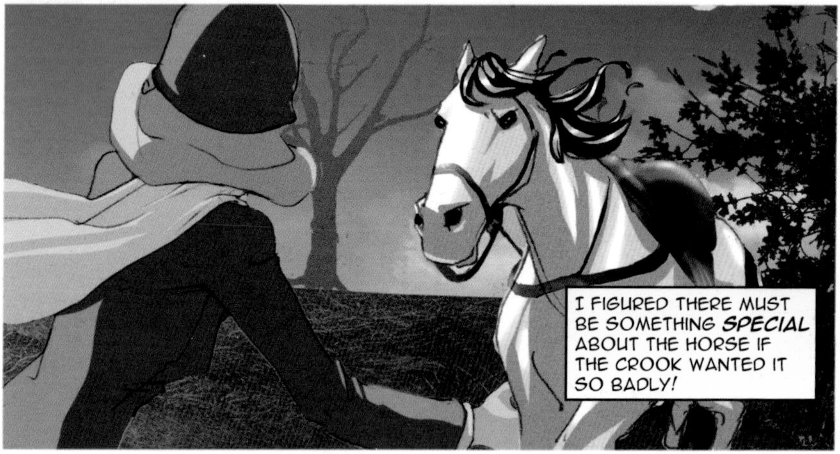
I FIGURED THERE MUST BE SOMETHING SPECIAL ABOUT THE HORSE IF THE CROOK WANTED IT SO BADLY!

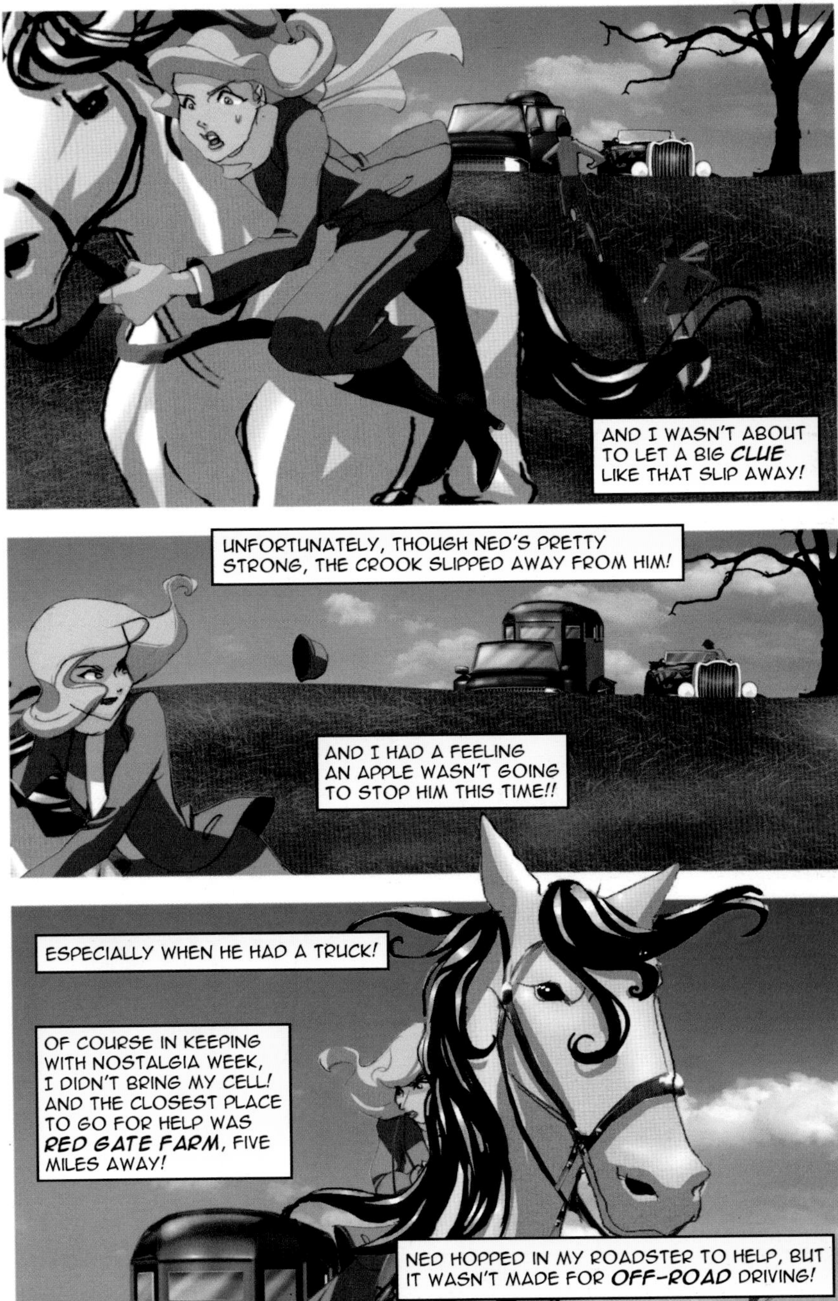
AND I WASN'T ABOUT TO LET A BIG CLUE LIKE THAT SLIP AWAY!
UNFORTUNATELY, THOUGH NED'S PRETTY STRONG, THE CROOK SLIPPED AWAY FROM HIM!
AND I HAD A FEELING AN APPLE WASN'T GOING TO STOP HIM THIS TIME!!
ESPECIALLY WHEN HE HAD A TRUCK!
OF COURSE IN KEEPING WITH NOSTALGIA WEEK, I DIDN'T BRING MY CELL! AND THE CLOSEST PLACE TO GO FOR HELP WAS RED GATE FARM, FIVE MILES AWAY!
NED HOPPED IN MY ROADSTER TO HELP, BUT IT WASN'T MADE FOR OFF-ROAD DRIVING!

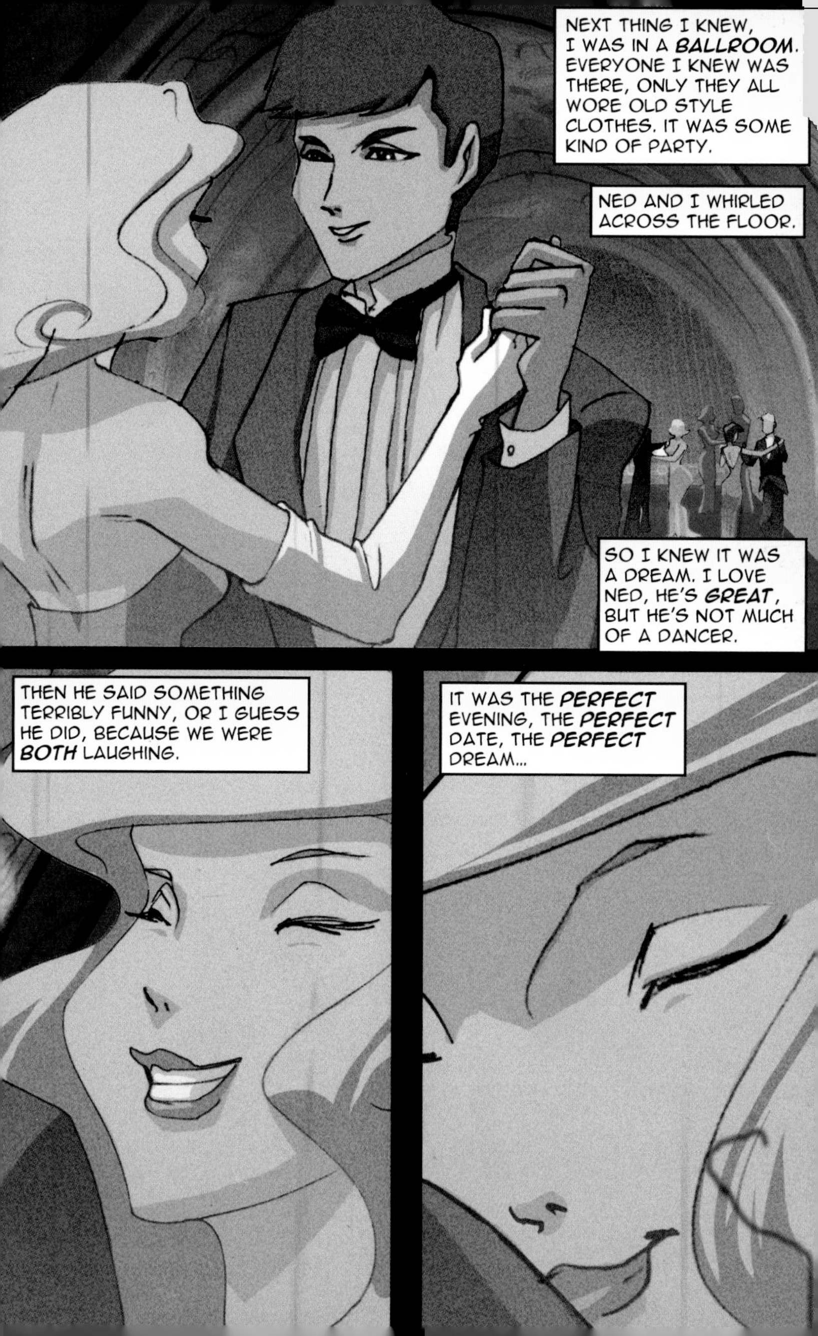
NEXT THING I KNEW, I WAS IN A BALLROOM. EVERYONE I KNEW WAS THERE, ONLY THEY ALL WORE OLD STYLE CLOTHES. IT WAS SOME KIND OF PARTY.
NED AND I WHIRLED ACROSS THE FLOOR.
SO I KNEW IT WAS A DREAM. I LOVE NED, HE'S GREAT, BUT HE'S NOT MUCH OF A DANCER.
THEN HE SAID SOMETHING TERRIBLY FUNNY, OR I GUESS HE DID, BECAUSE WE WERE BOTH LAUGHING.
IT WAS THE PERFECT EVENING, THE PERFECT DATE, THE PERFECT DREAM...

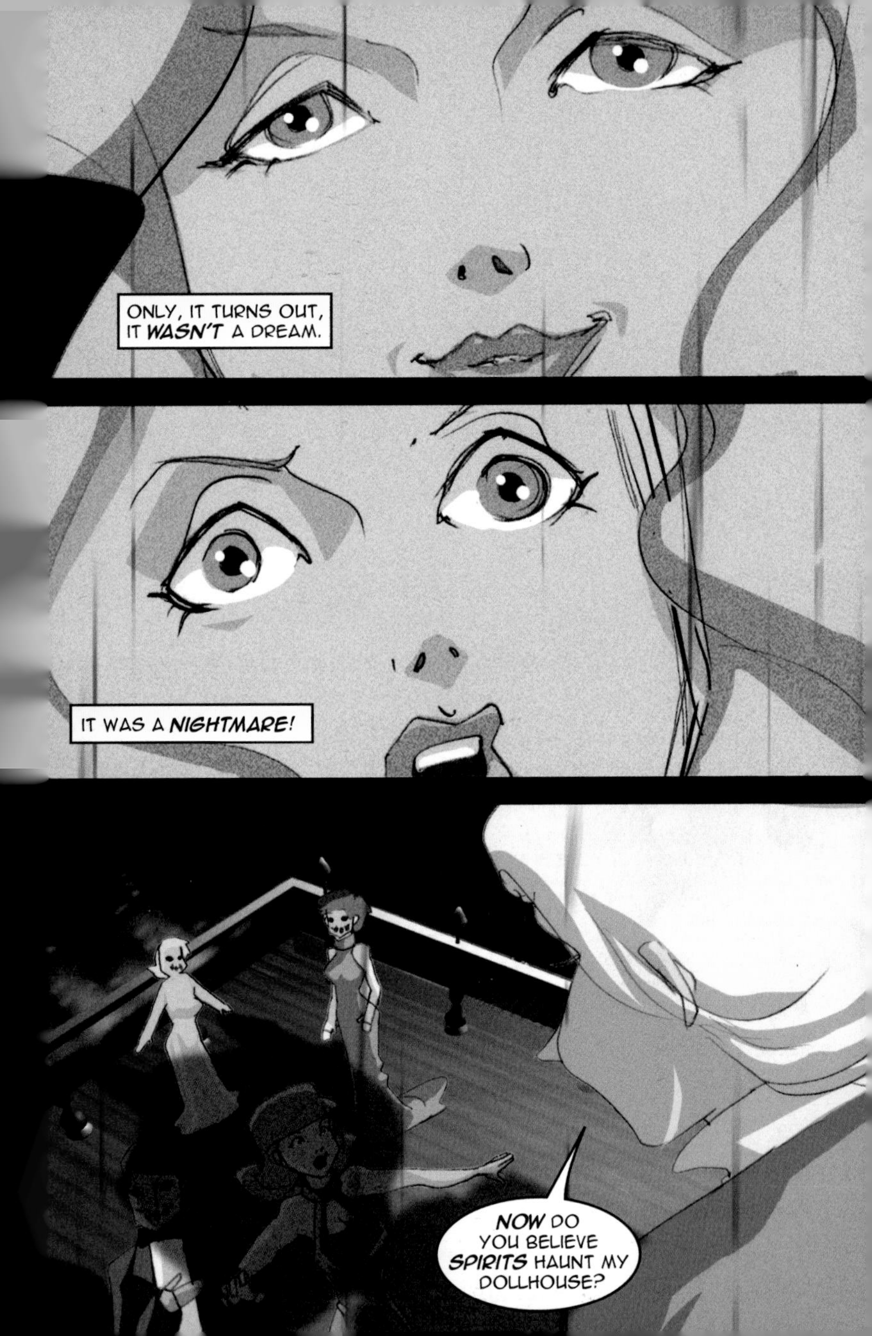
ONLY, IT TURNS OUT, IT WASN'T A DREAM.
IT WAS A NIGHTMARE!
NOW DO YOU BELIEVE SPIRITS HAUNT MY DOLLHOUSE?

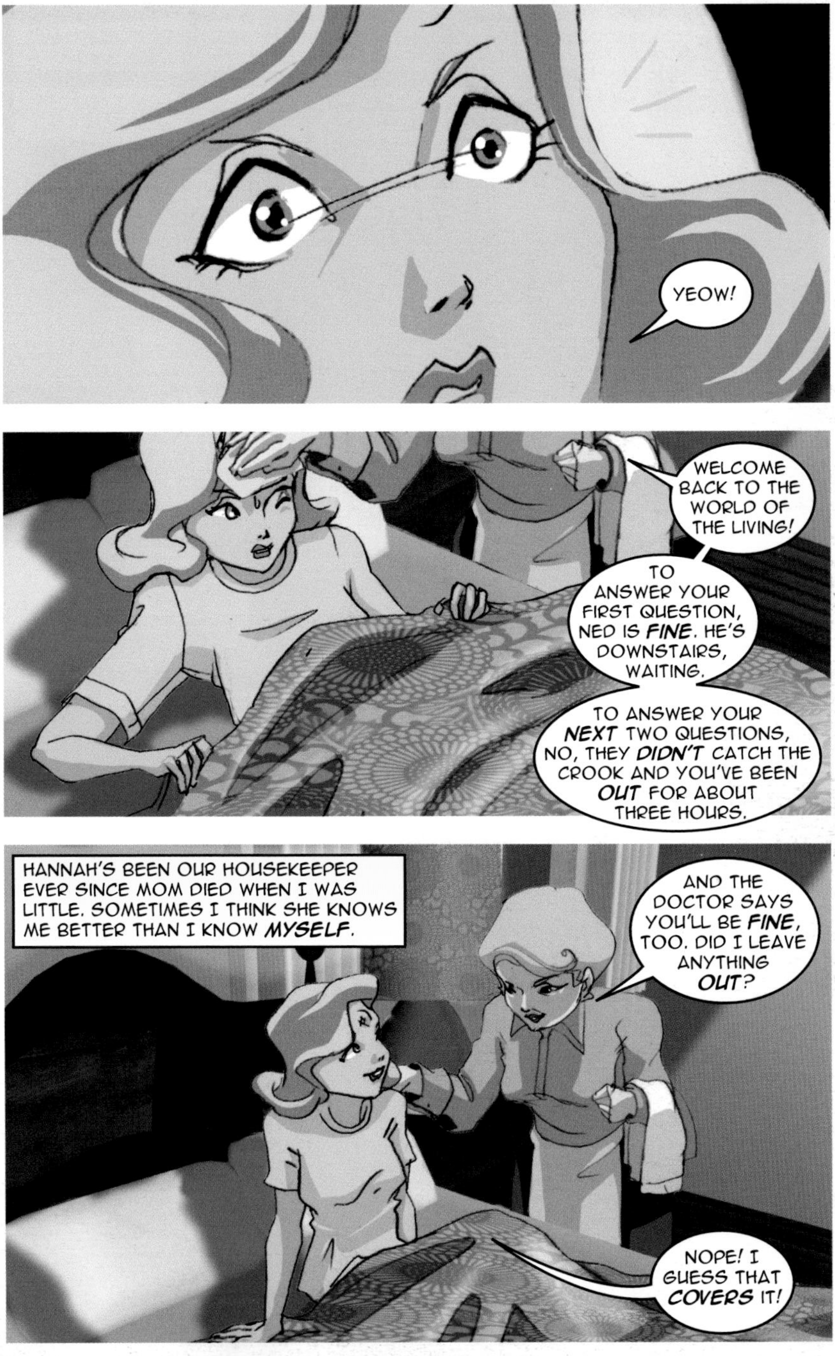
YEOW!
WELCOME BACK TO THE WORLD OF THE LIVING!
TO ANSWER YOUR FIRST QUESTION, NED IS FINE. HE'S DOWNSTAIRS, WAITING.
TO ANSWER YOUR NEXT TWO QUESTIONS, NO, THEY DIDN'T CATCH THE CROOK AND YOU'VE BEEN OUT FOR ABOUT THREE HOURS.
HANNAH'S BEEN OUR HOUSEKEEPER EVER SINCE MOM DIED WHEN I WAS LITTLE. SOMETIMES I THINK SHE KNOWS ME BETTER THAN I KNOW MYSELF.
AND THE DOCTOR SAYS YOU'LL BE FINE, TOO. DID I LEAVE ANYTHING OUT?
NOPE! I GUESS THAT COVERS IT!

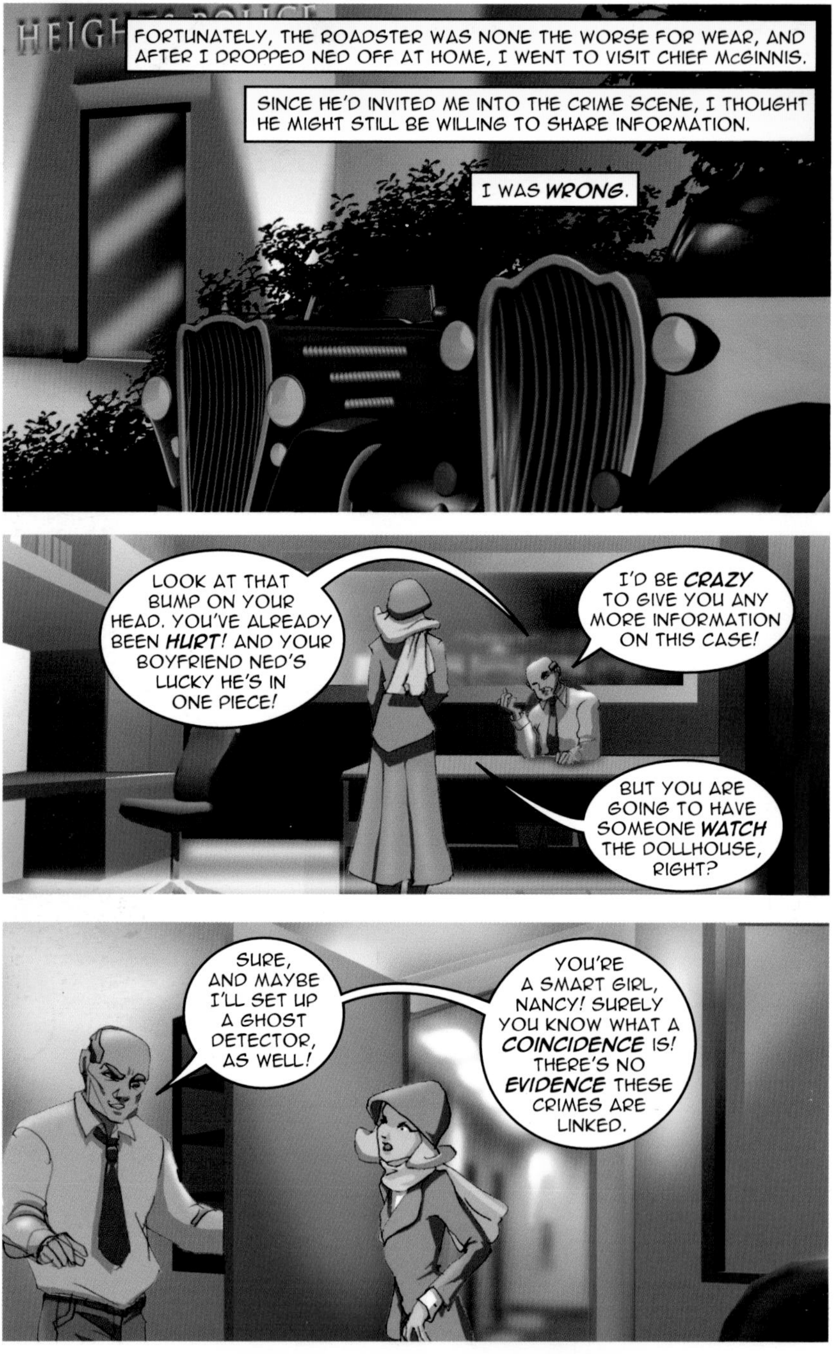
HEIGH
FORTUNATELY, THE ROADSTER WAS NONE THE WORSE FOR WEAR, AND AFTER I DROPPED NED OFF AT HOME, I WENT TO VISIT CHIEF McGINNIS.
SINCE HE'D INVITED ME INTO THE CRIME SCENE, I THOUGHT HE MIGHT STILL BE WILLING TO SHARE INFORMATION.
I WAS WRONG.
LOOK AT THAT BUMP ON YOUR HEAD. YOU'VE ALREADY BEEN HURT! AND YOUR BOYFRIEND NED'S LUCKY HE'S IN ONE PIECE!
I'D BE CRAZY TO GIVE YOU ANY MORE INFORMATION ON THIS CASE!
BUT YOU ARE GOING TO HAVE SOMEONE WATCH THE DOLLHOUSE, RIGHT?
SURE, AND MAYBE I'LL SET UP A GHOST DETECTOR, AS WELL!
YOU'RE A SMART GIRL, NANCY! SURELY YOU KNOW WHAT A COINCIDENCE IS! THERE'S NO EVIDENCE THESE CRIMES ARE LINKED.

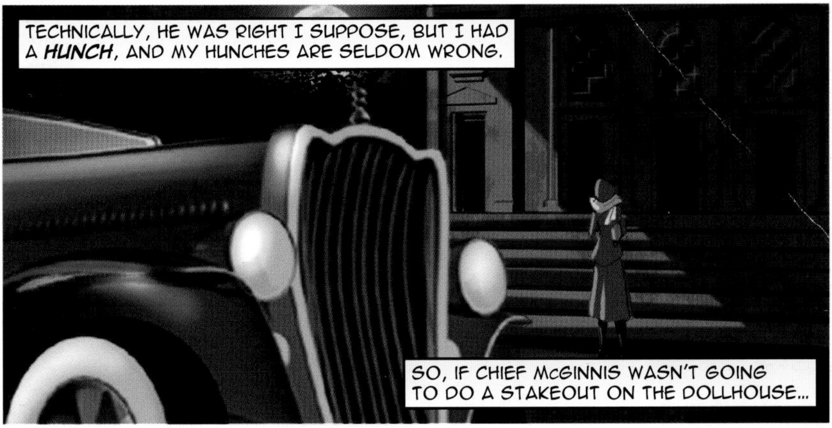
TECHNICALLY, HE WAS RIGHT I SUPPOSE, BUT I HAD A HUNCH, AND MY HUNCHES ARE SELDOM WRONG.
SO, IF CHIEF McGINNIS WASN'T GOING TO DO A STAKEOUT ON THE DOLLHOUSE...

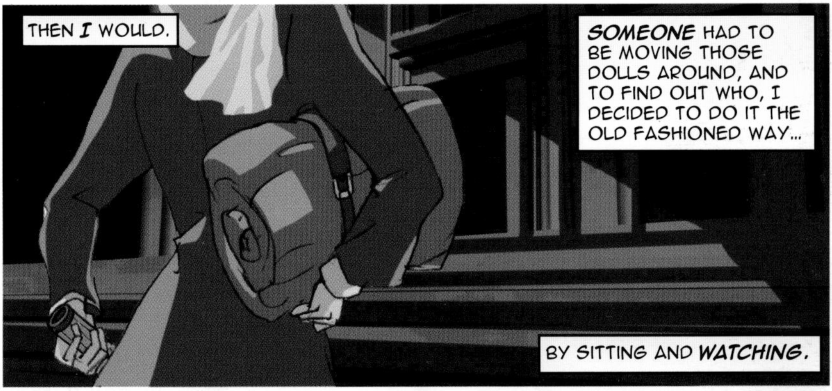
THEN I WOULD.
SOMEONE HAD TO BE MOVING THOSE DOLLS AROUND, AND TO FIND OUT WHO, I DECIDED TO DO IT THE OLD FASHIONED WAY...
BY SITTING AND WATCHING.

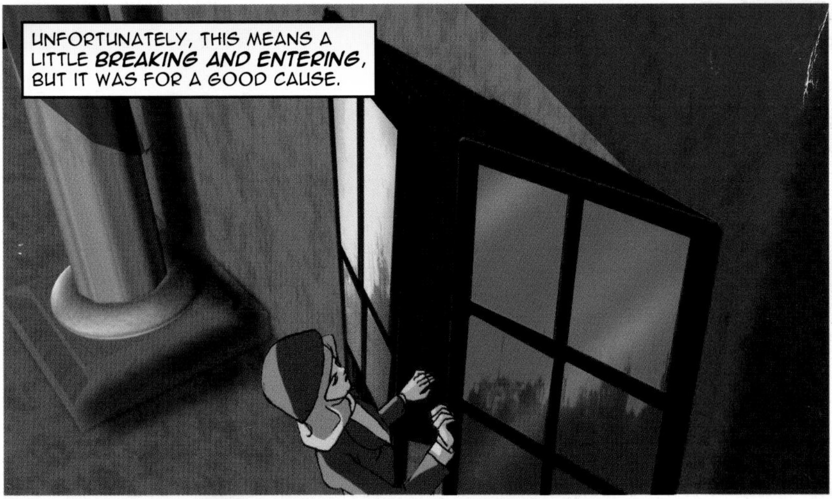
UNFORTUNATELY, THIS MEANS A LITTLE BREAKING AND ENTERING, BUT IT WAS FOR A GOOD CAUSE.

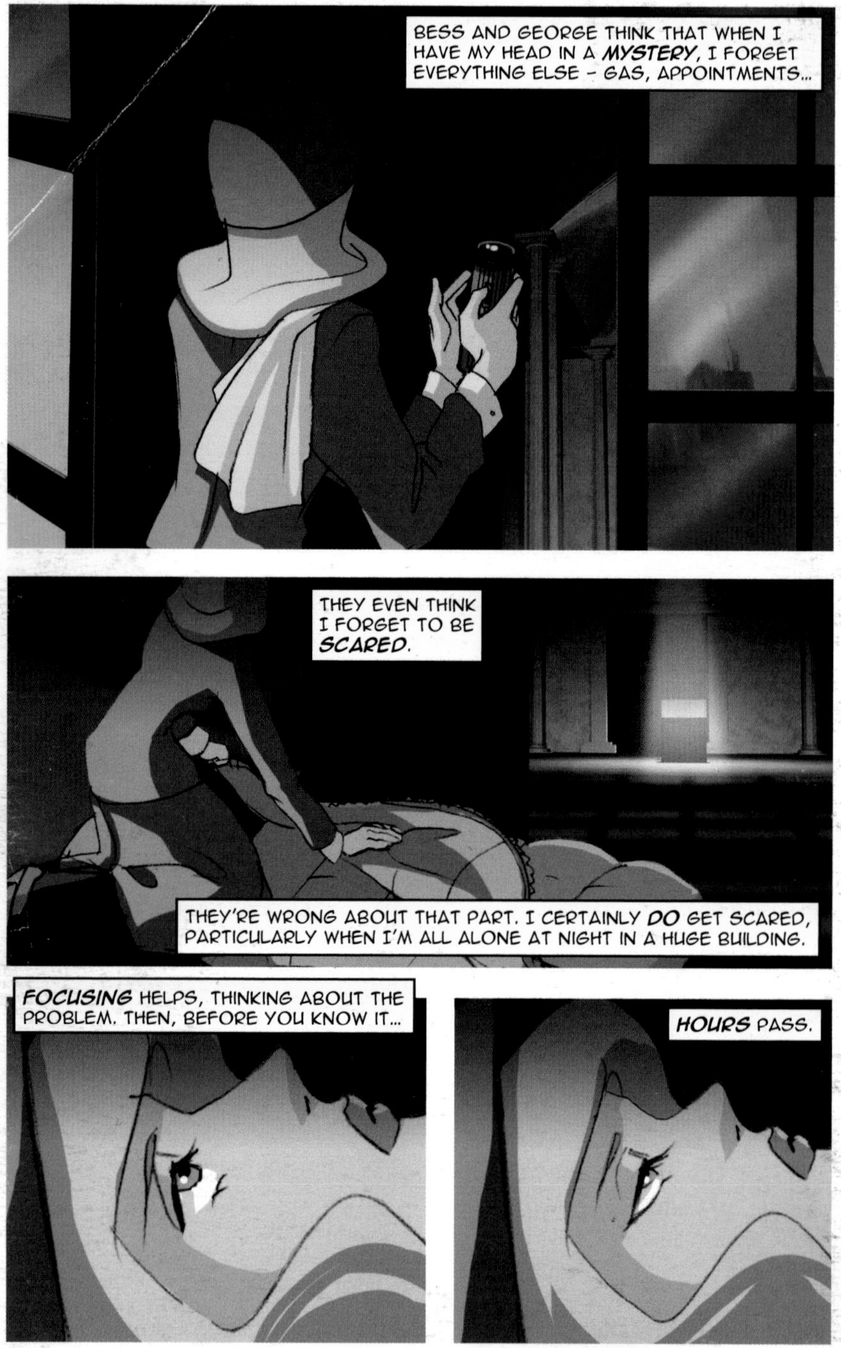
BESS AND GEORGE THINK THAT WHEN I HAVE MY HEAD IN A *MYSTERY*, I FORGET EVERYTHING ELSE - GAS, APPOINTMENTS...
THEY EVEN THINK I FORGET TO BE *SCARED*.
THEY'RE WRONG ABOUT THAT PART. I CERTAINLY *DO* GET SCARED, PARTICULARLY WHEN I'M ALL ALONE AT NIGHT IN A HUGE BUILDING.
FOCUSING HELPS, THINKING ABOUT THE PROBLEM. THEN, BEFORE YOU KNOW IT...
HOURS PASS.

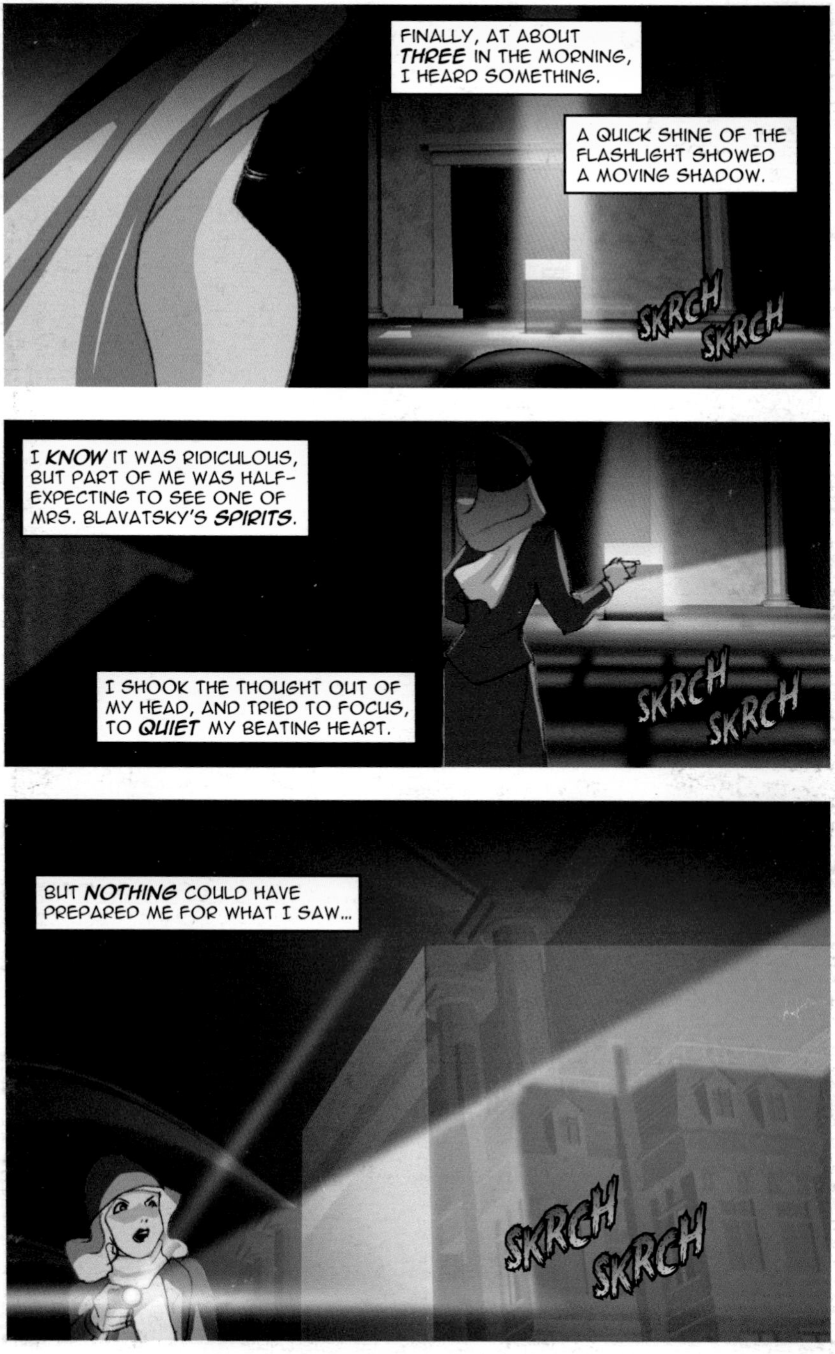
FINALLY, AT ABOUT THREE IN THE MORNING, I HEARD SOMETHING.
A QUICK SHINE OF THE FLASHLIGHT SHOWED A MOVING SHADOW.
SKRCH SKRCH
I KNOW IT WAS RIDICULOUS, BUT PART OF ME WAS HALF-EXPECTING TO SEE ONE OF MRS. BLAVATSKY'S SPIRITS.
I SHOOK THE THOUGHT OUT OF MY HEAD, AND TRIED TO FOCUS, TO QUIET MY BEATING HEART.
SKRCH SKRCH
BUT NOTHING COULD HAVE PREPARED ME FOR WHAT I SAW...
SKRCH SKRCH

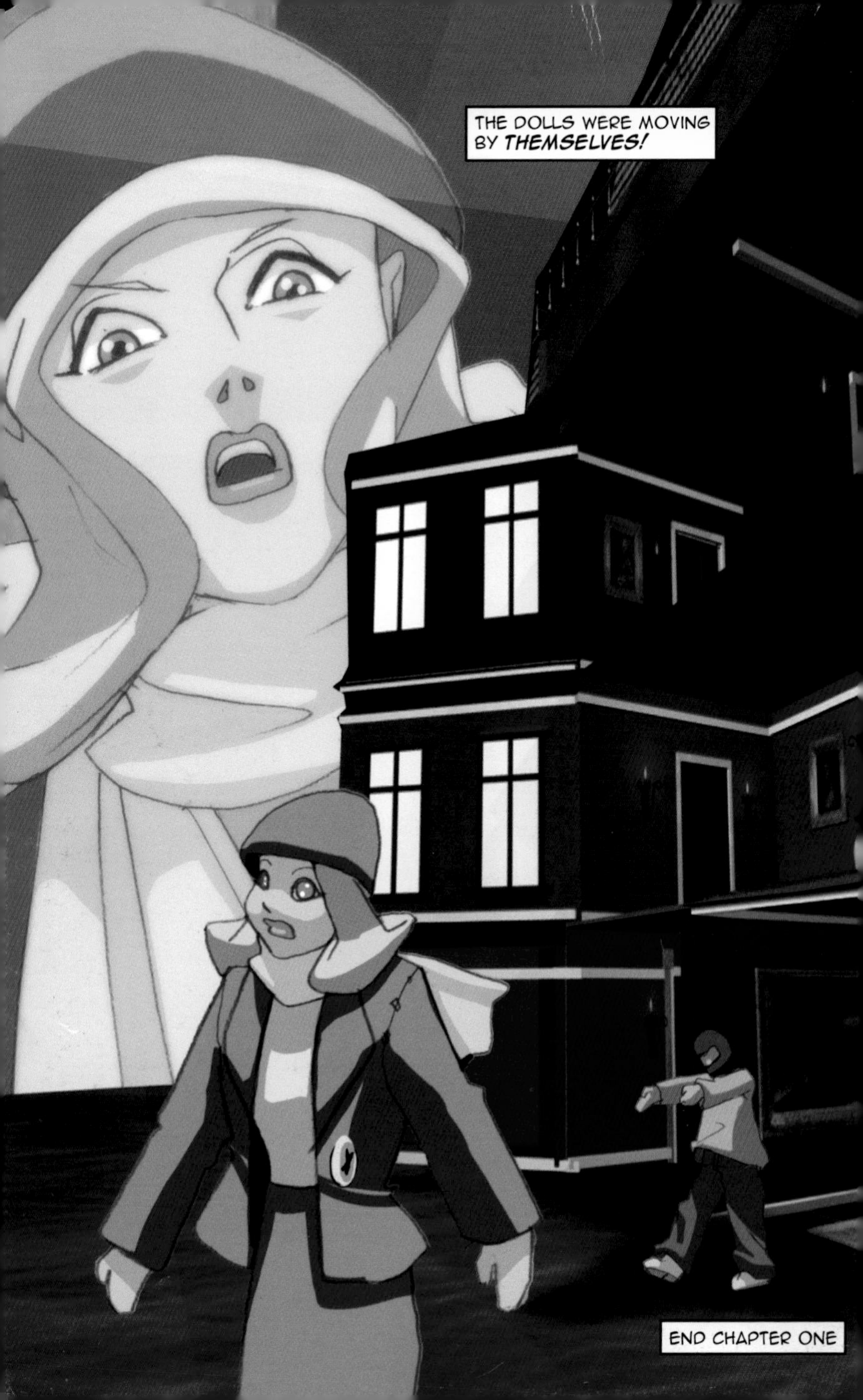
THE DOLLS WERE MOVING BY THEMSELVES!
END CHAPTER ONE

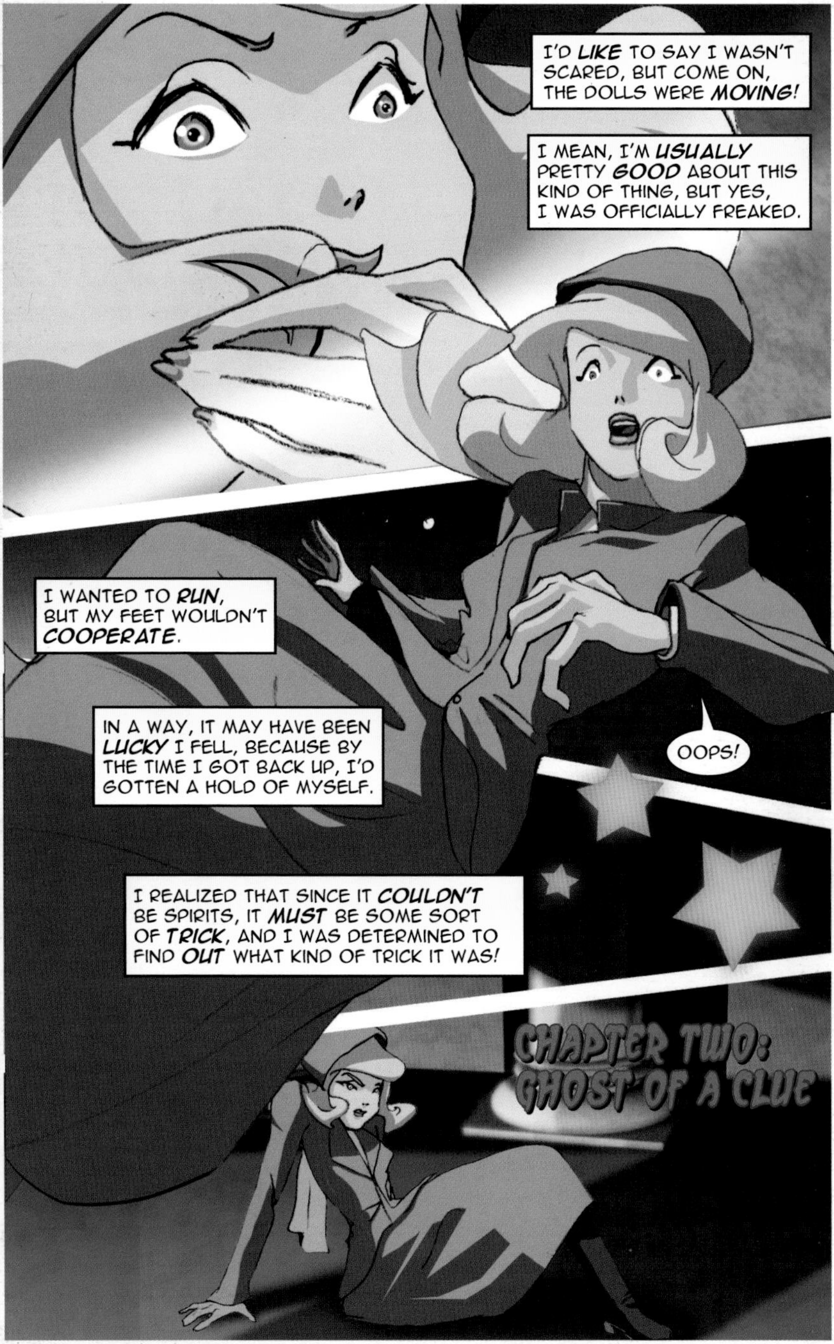
I'D LIKE TO SAY I WASN'T SCARED, BUT COME ON, THE DOLLS WERE MOVING!
I MEAN, I'M USUALLY PRETTY GOOD ABOUT THIS KIND OF THING, BUT YES, I WAS OFFICIALLY FREAKED.
I WANTED TO RUN, BUT MY FEET WOULDN'T COOPERATE.
IN A WAY, IT MAY HAVE BEEN LUCKY I FELL, BECAUSE BY THE TIME I GOT BACK UP, I'D GOTTEN A HOLD OF MYSELF.
OOPS!
I REALIZED THAT SINCE IT COULDN'T BE SPIRITS, IT MUST BE SOME SORT OF TRICK, AND I WAS DETERMINED TO FIND OUT WHAT KIND OF TRICK IT WAS!
CHAPTER TWO: GHOST OF A CLUE

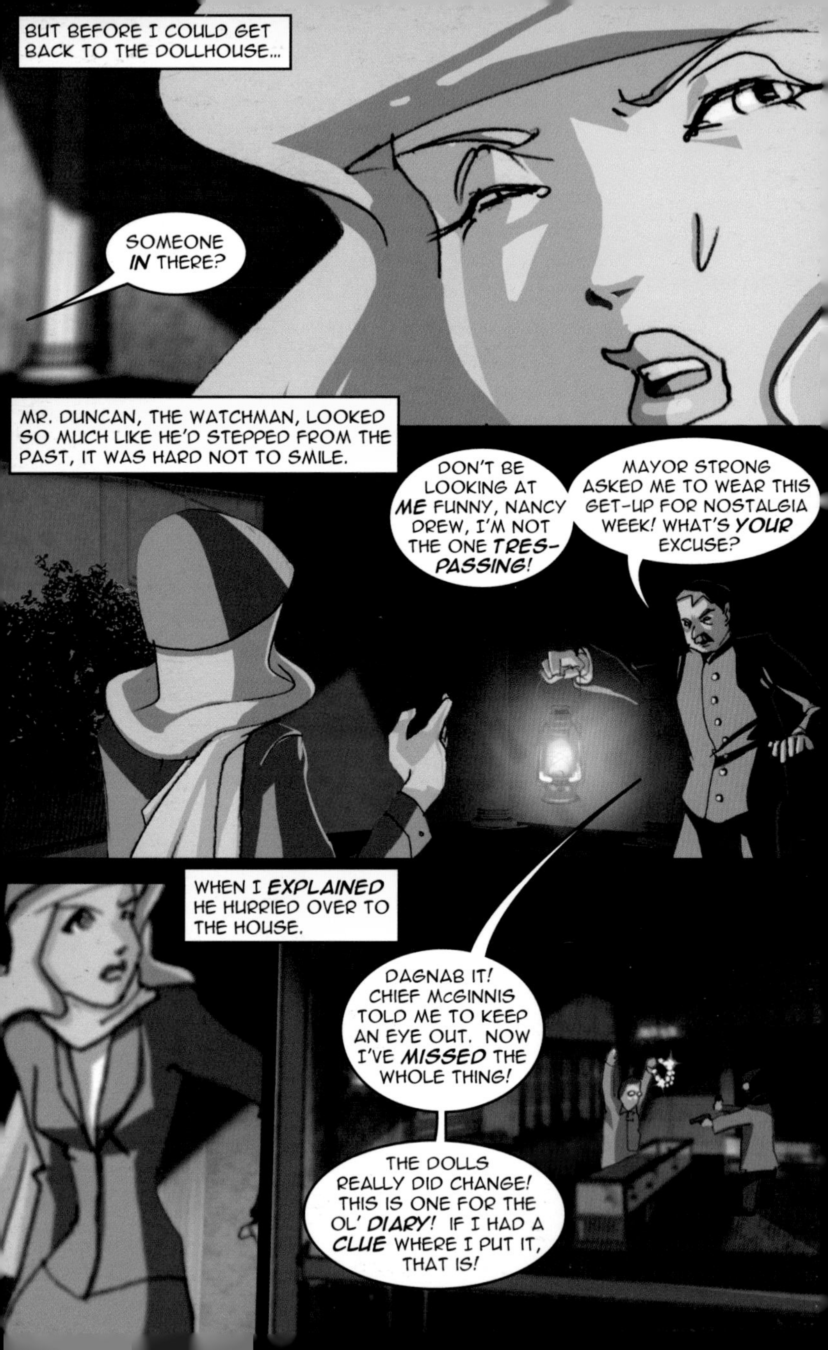
BUT BEFORE I COULD GET BACK TO THE DOLLHOUSE...
SOMEONE *IN* THERE?
MR. DUNCAN, THE WATCHMAN, LOOKED SO MUCH LIKE HE'D STEPPED FROM THE PAST, IT WAS HARD NOT TO SMILE.
DON'T BE LOOKING AT *ME* FUNNY, NANCY DREW, I'M NOT THE ONE *TRES-PASSING*!
MAYOR STRONG ASKED ME TO WEAR THIS GET-UP FOR NOSTALGIA WEEK! WHAT'S *YOUR* EXCUSE?
WHEN I *EXPLAINED* HE HURRIED OVER TO THE HOUSE.
DAGNAB IT! CHIEF McGINNIS TOLD ME TO KEEP AN EYE OUT. NOW I'VE *MISSED* THE WHOLE THING!
THE DOLLS REALLY DID CHANGE! THIS IS ONE FOR THE OL' *DIARY*! IF I HAD A *CLUE* WHERE I PUT IT, THAT IS!

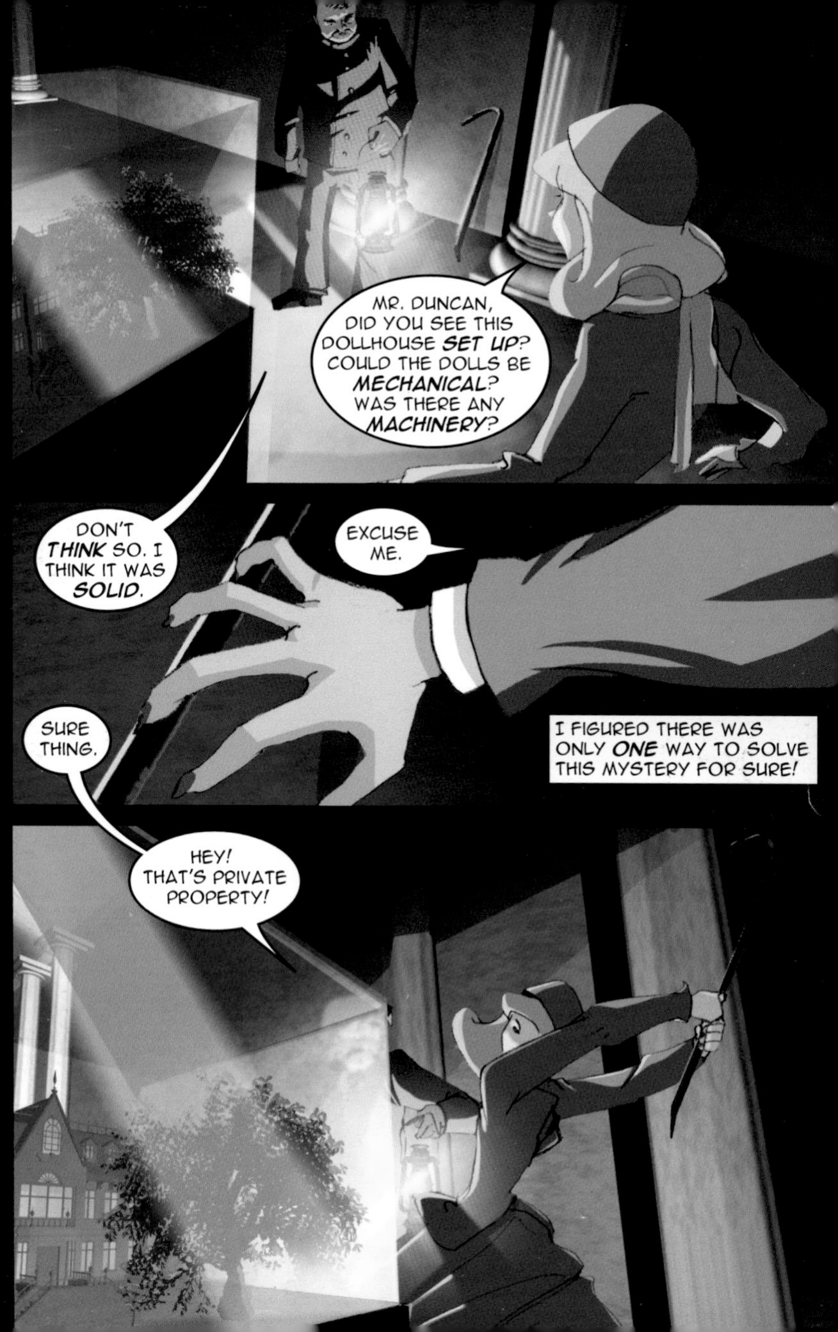
MR. DUNCAN, DID YOU SEE THIS DOLLHOUSE SET UP? COULD THE DOLLS BE MECHANICAL? WAS THERE ANY MACHINERY?
DON'T THINK SO. I THINK IT WAS SOLID.
EXCUSE ME.
SURE THING.
I FIGURED THERE WAS ONLY ONE WAY TO SOLVE THIS MYSTERY FOR SURE!
HEY! THAT'S PRIVATE PROPERTY!

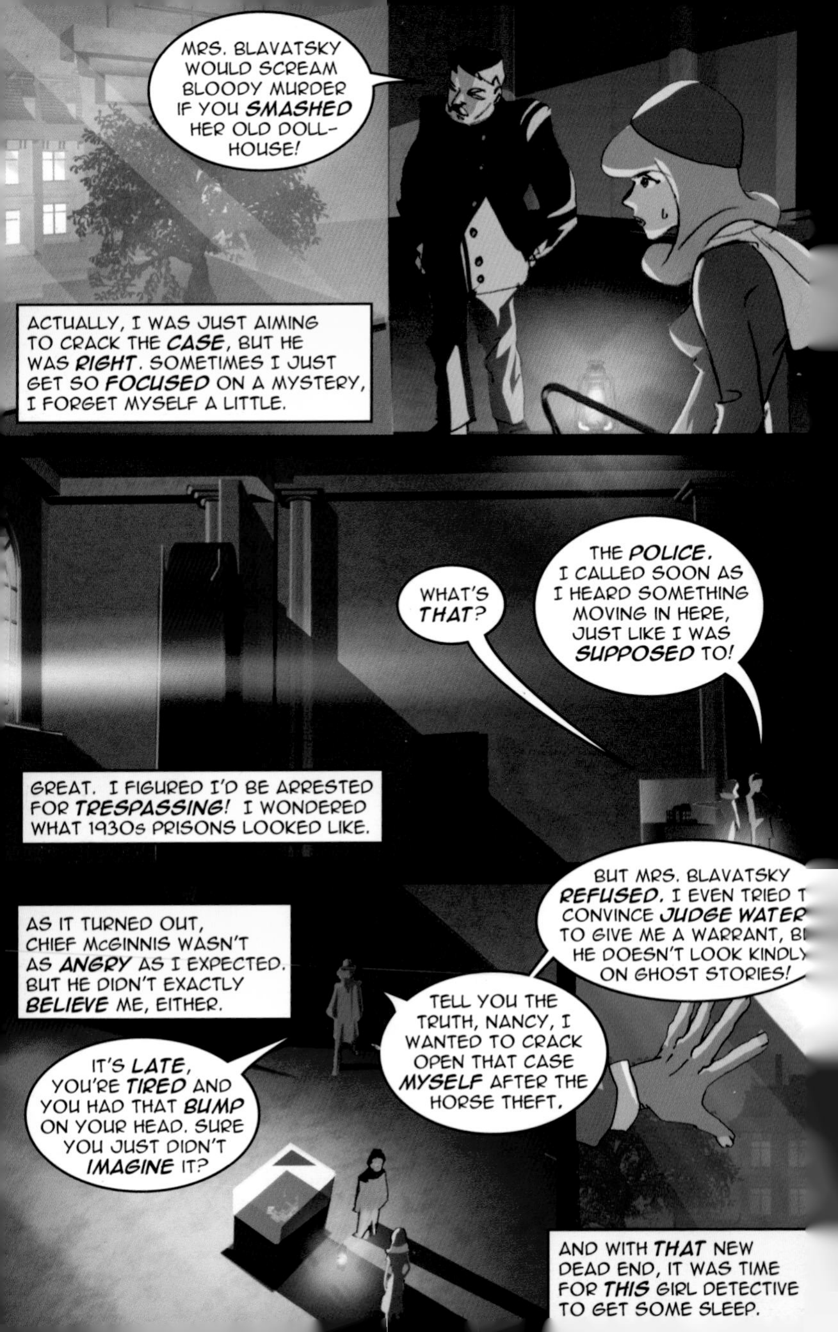

MRS. BLAVATSKY WOULD SCREAM BLOODY MURDER IF YOU SMASHED HER OLD DOLL-HOUSE!
ACTUALLY, I WAS JUST AIMING TO CRACK THE CASE, BUT HE WAS RIGHT. SOMETIMES I JUST GET SO FOCUSED ON A MYSTERY, I FORGET MYSELF A LITTLE.
WHAT'S THAT?
THE POLICE. I CALLED SOON AS I HEARD SOMETHING MOVING IN HERE, JUST LIKE I WAS SUPPOSED TO!
GREAT. I FIGURED I'D BE ARRESTED FOR TRESPASSING! I WONDERED WHAT 1930s PRISONS LOOKED LIKE.
AS IT TURNED OUT, CHIEF McGINNIS WASN'T AS ANGRY AS I EXPECTED. BUT HE DIDN'T EXACTLY BELIEVE ME, EITHER.
IT'S LATE, YOU'RE TIRED AND YOU HAD THAT BUMP ON YOUR HEAD. SURE YOU JUST DIDN'T IMAGINE IT?
TELL YOU THE TRUTH, NANCY, I WANTED TO CRACK OPEN THAT CASE MYSELF AFTER THE HORSE THEFT.
BUT MRS. BLAVATSKY REFUSED. I EVEN TRIED T CONVINCE JUDGE WATER TO GIVE ME A WARRANT, B HE DOESN'T LOOK KINDL ON GHOST STORIES!
AND WITH THAT NEW DEAD END, IT WAS TIME FOR THIS GIRL DETECTIVE TO GET SOME SLEEP.

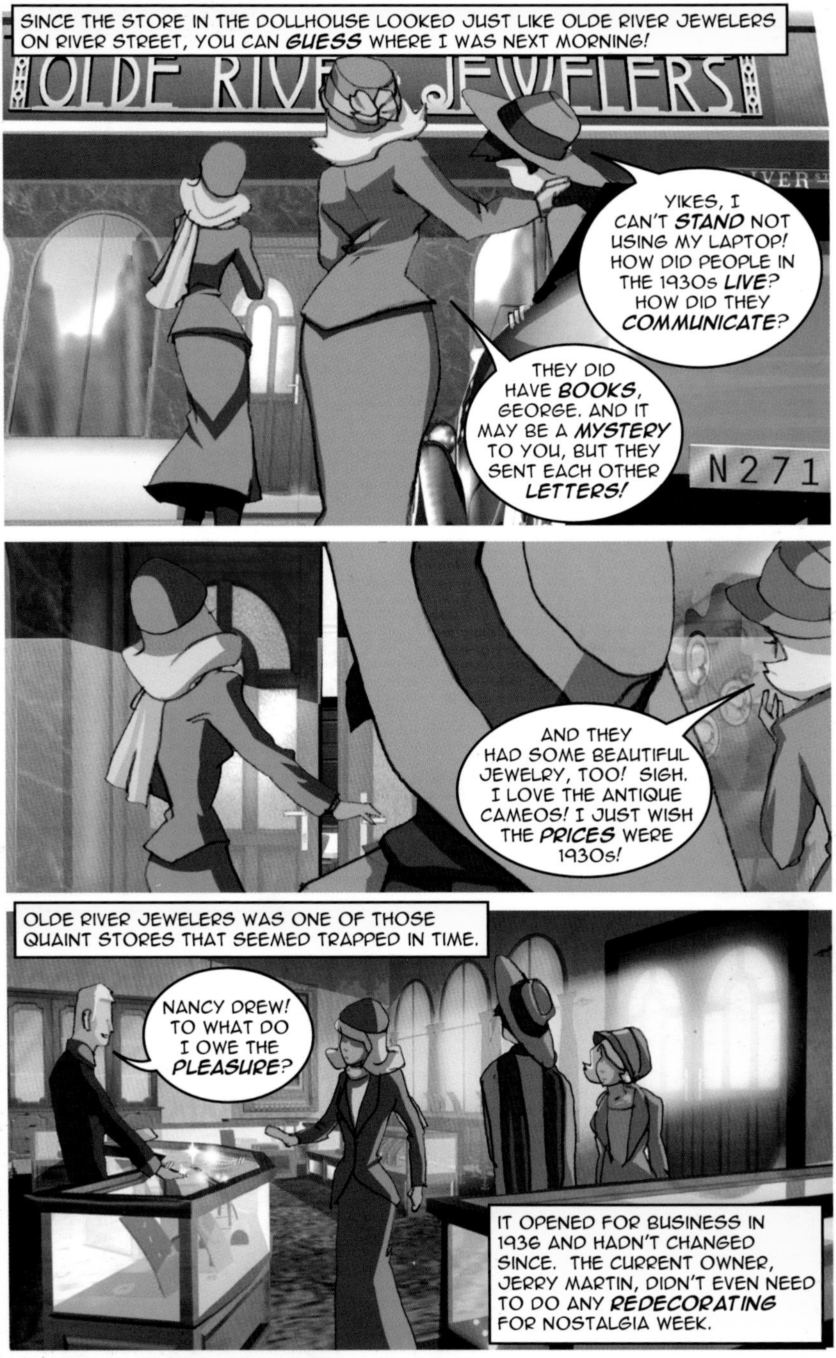
SINCE THE STORE IN THE DOLLHOUSE LOOKED JUST LIKE OLDE RIVER JEWELERS ON RIVER STREET, YOU CAN *GUESS* WHERE I WAS NEXT MORNING!
OLDE RIVER JEWELERS
YIKES, I CAN'T *STAND* NOT USING MY LAPTOP! HOW DID PEOPLE IN THE 1930s *LIVE*? HOW DID THEY *COMMUNICATE*?
THEY DID HAVE *BOOKS*, GEORGE. AND IT MAY BE A *MYSTERY* TO YOU, BUT THEY SENT EACH OTHER *LETTERS!*
N 271
AND THEY HAD SOME BEAUTIFUL JEWELRY, TOO! SIGH. I LOVE THE ANTIQUE CAMEOS! I JUST WISH THE *PRICES* WERE 1930s!
OLDE RIVER JEWELERS WAS ONE OF THOSE QUAINT STORES THAT SEEMED TRAPPED IN TIME.
NANCY DREW! TO WHAT DO I OWE THE *PLEASURE*?
IT OPENED FOR BUSINESS IN 1936 AND HADN'T CHANGED SINCE. THE CURRENT OWNER, JERRY MARTIN, DIDN'T EVEN NEED TO DO ANY *REDECORATING* FOR NOSTALGIA WEEK.

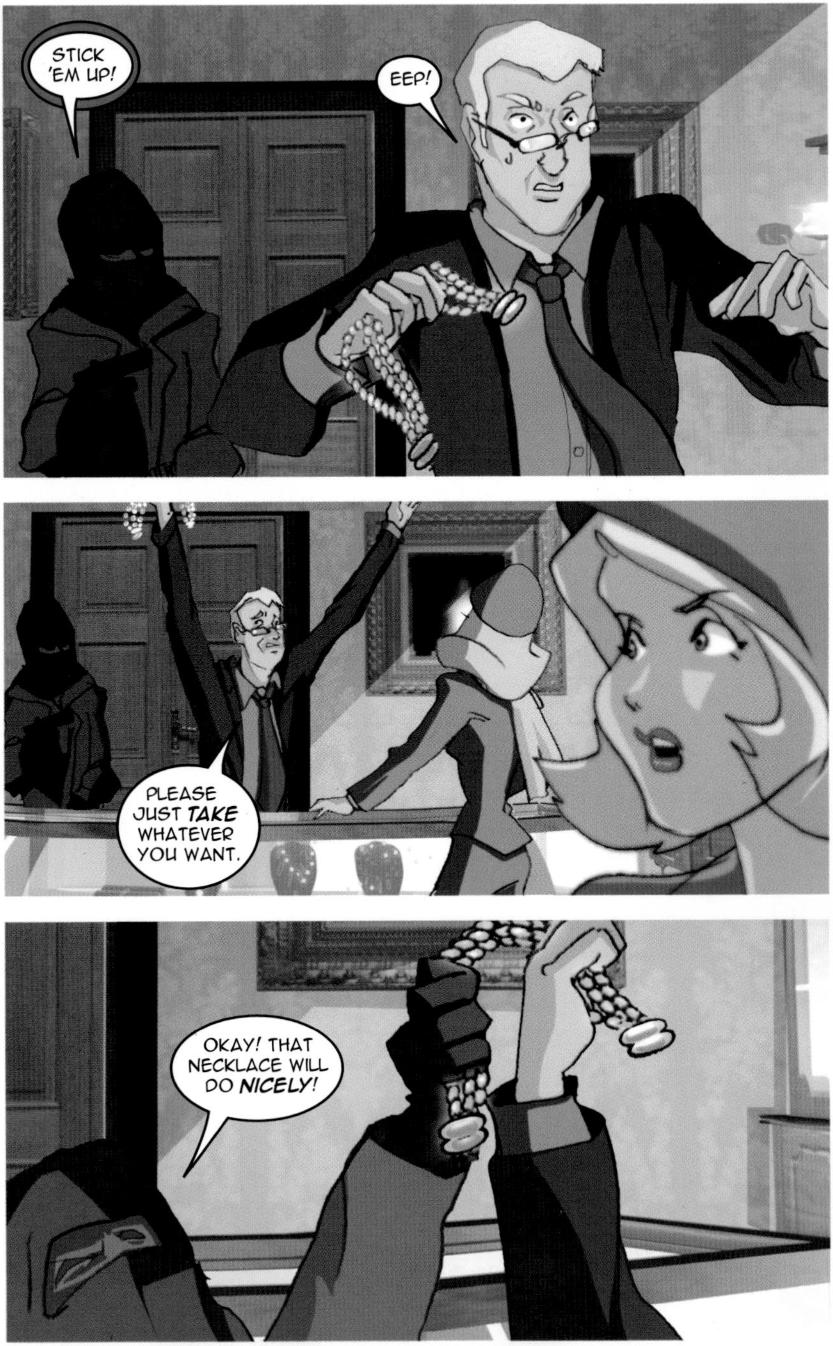
STICK 'EM UP!
EEP!
PLEASE JUST **TAKE** WHATEVER YOU WANT.
OKAY! THAT NECKLACE WILL DO **NICELY**!

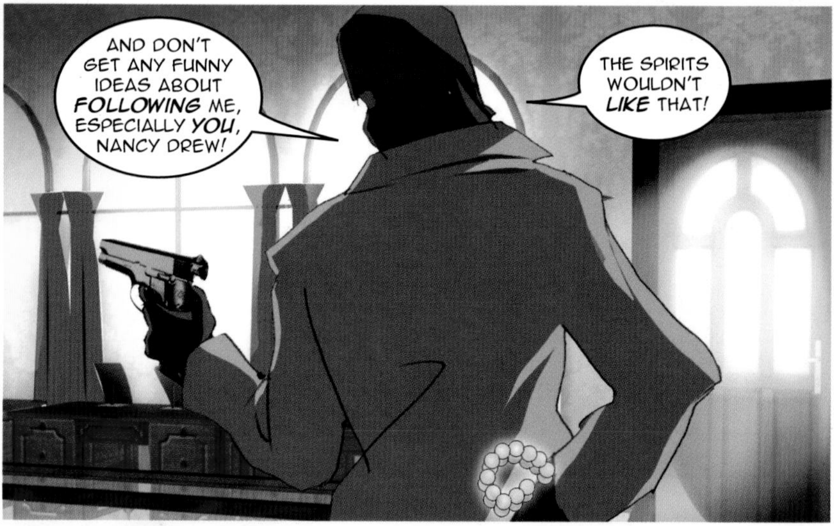
AND DON'T GET ANY FUNNY IDEAS ABOUT FOLLOWING ME, ESPECIALLY YOU, NANCY DREW!
THE SPIRITS WOULDN'T LIKE THAT!

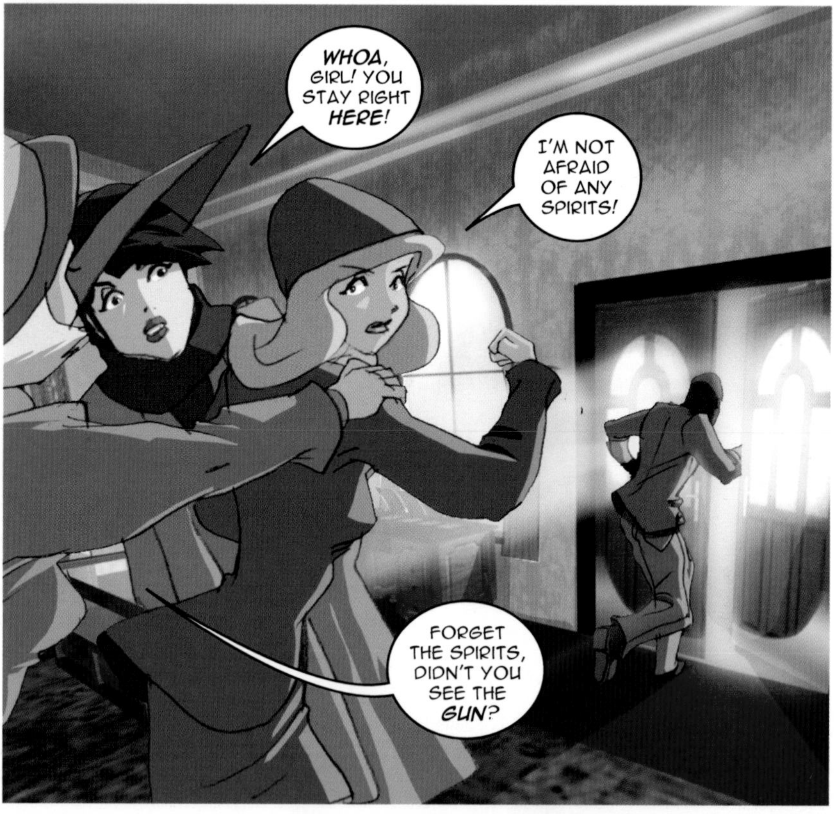
WHOA, GIRL! YOU STAY RIGHT HERE!
I'M NOT AFRAID OF ANY SPIRITS!
FORGET THE SPIRITS, DIDN'T YOU SEE THE GUN?

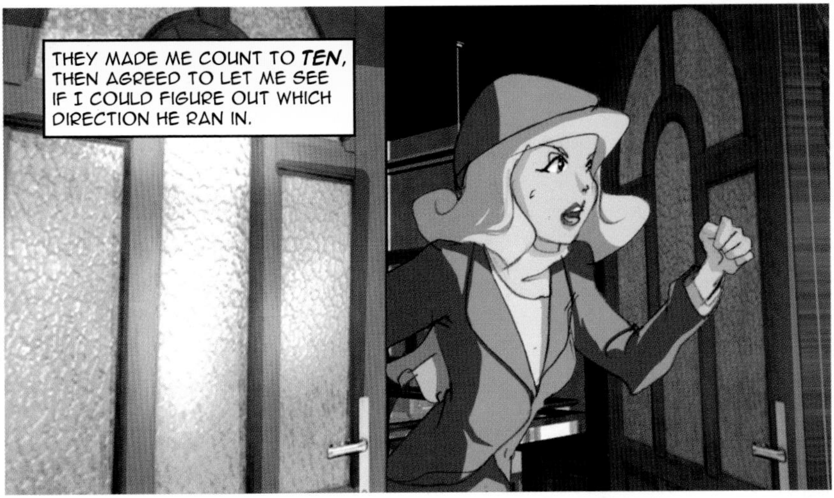
THEY MADE ME COUNT TO **TEN**, THEN AGREED TO LET ME SEE IF I COULD FIGURE OUT WHICH DIRECTION HE RAN IN.

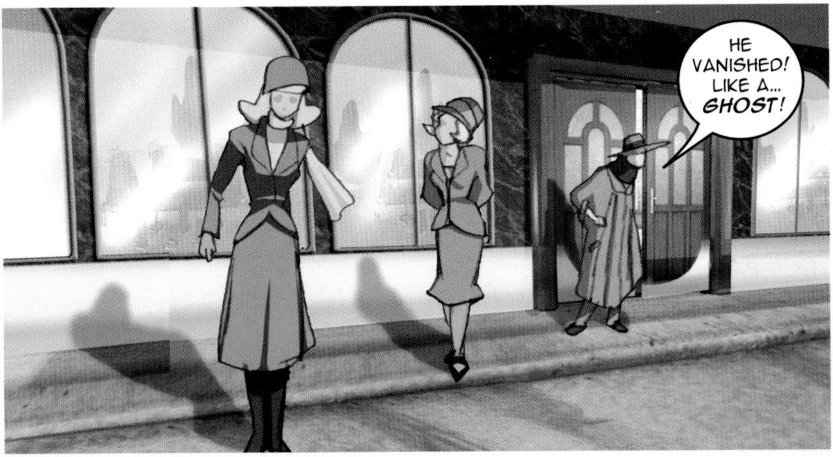
HE VANISHED! LIKE A... **GHOST**!

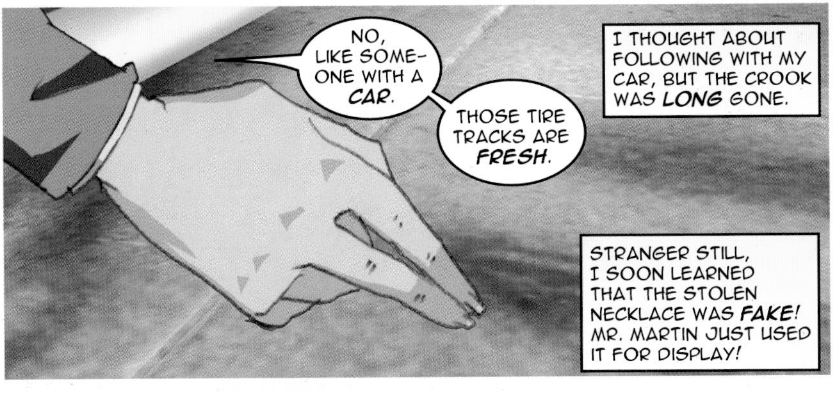
NO, LIKE SOME-ONE WITH A **CAR**.
THOSE TIRE TRACKS ARE **FRESH**.
I THOUGHT ABOUT FOLLOWING WITH MY CAR, BUT THE CROOK WAS **LONG** GONE.
STRANGER STILL, I SOON LEARNED THAT THE STOLEN NECKLACE WAS **FAKE**! MR. MARTIN JUST USED IT FOR DISPLAY!

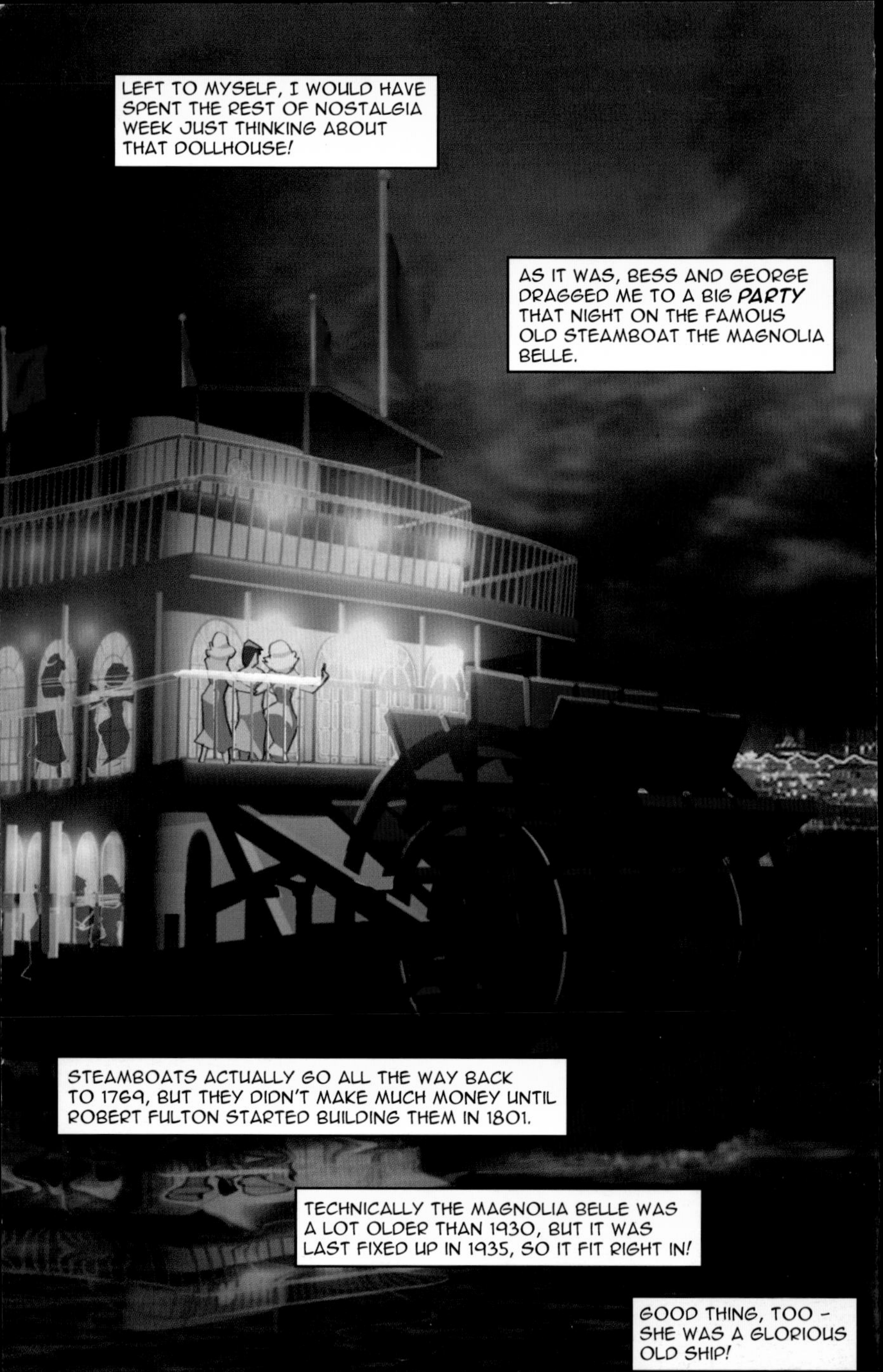
LEFT TO MYSELF, I WOULD HAVE SPENT THE REST OF NOSTALGIA WEEK JUST THINKING ABOUT THAT DOLLHOUSE!
AS IT WAS, BESS AND GEORGE DRAGGED ME TO A BIG PARTY THAT NIGHT ON THE FAMOUS OLD STEAMBOAT THE MAGNOLIA BELLE.
STEAMBOATS ACTUALLY GO ALL THE WAY BACK TO 1769, BUT THEY DIDN'T MAKE MUCH MONEY UNTIL ROBERT FULTON STARTED BUILDING THEM IN 1801.
TECHNICALLY THE MAGNOLIA BELLE WAS A LOT OLDER THAN 1930, BUT IT WAS LAST FIXED UP IN 1935, SO IT FIT RIGHT IN!
GOOD THING, TOO - SHE WAS A GLORIOUS OLD SHIP!

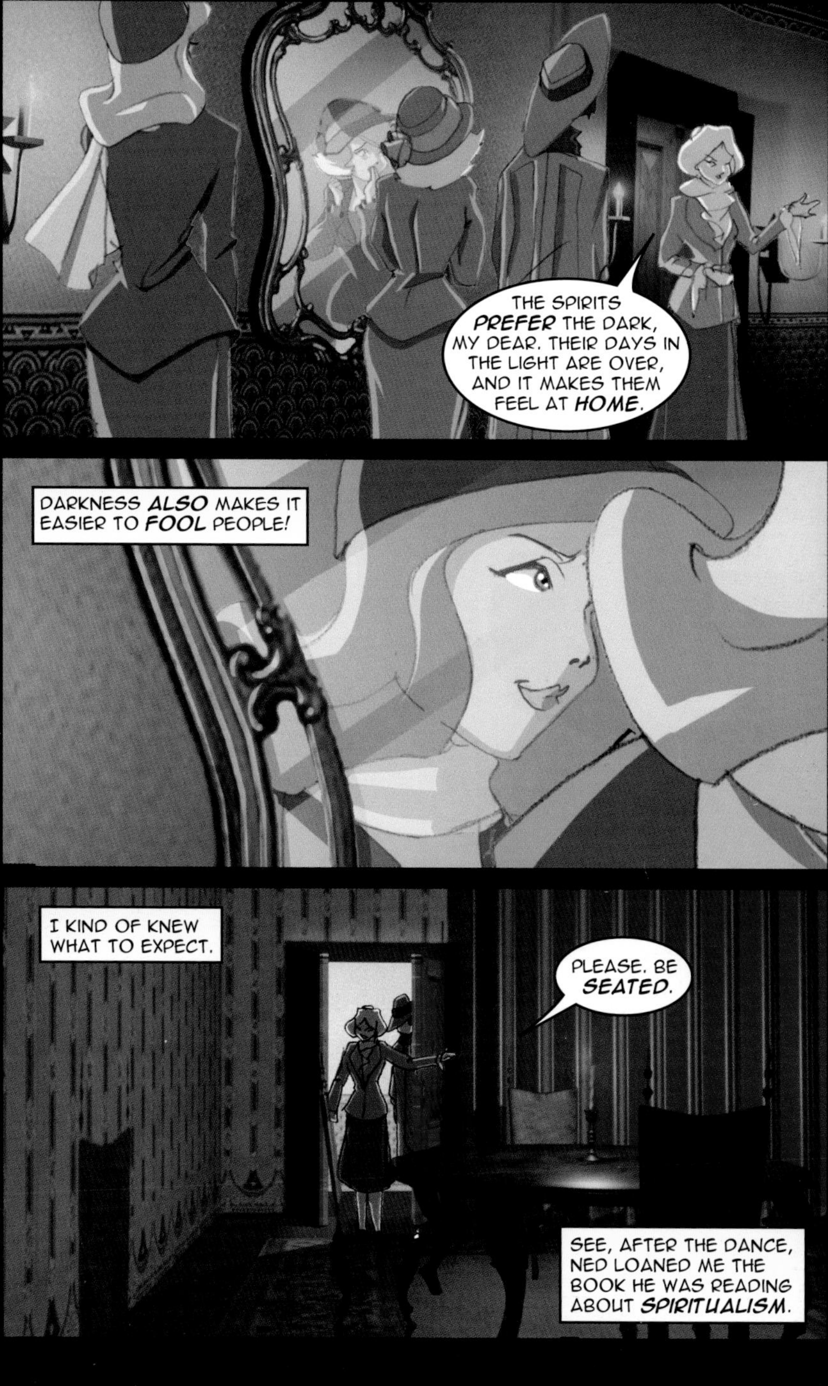
THE SPIRITS PREFER THE DARK, MY DEAR. THEIR DAYS IN THE LIGHT ARE OVER, AND IT MAKES THEM FEEL AT HOME.
DARKNESS ALSO MAKES IT EASIER TO FOOL PEOPLE!
I KIND OF KNEW WHAT TO EXPECT.
PLEASE. BE SEATED.
SEE, AFTER THE DANCE, NED LOANED ME THE BOOK HE WAS READING ABOUT SPIRITUALISM.

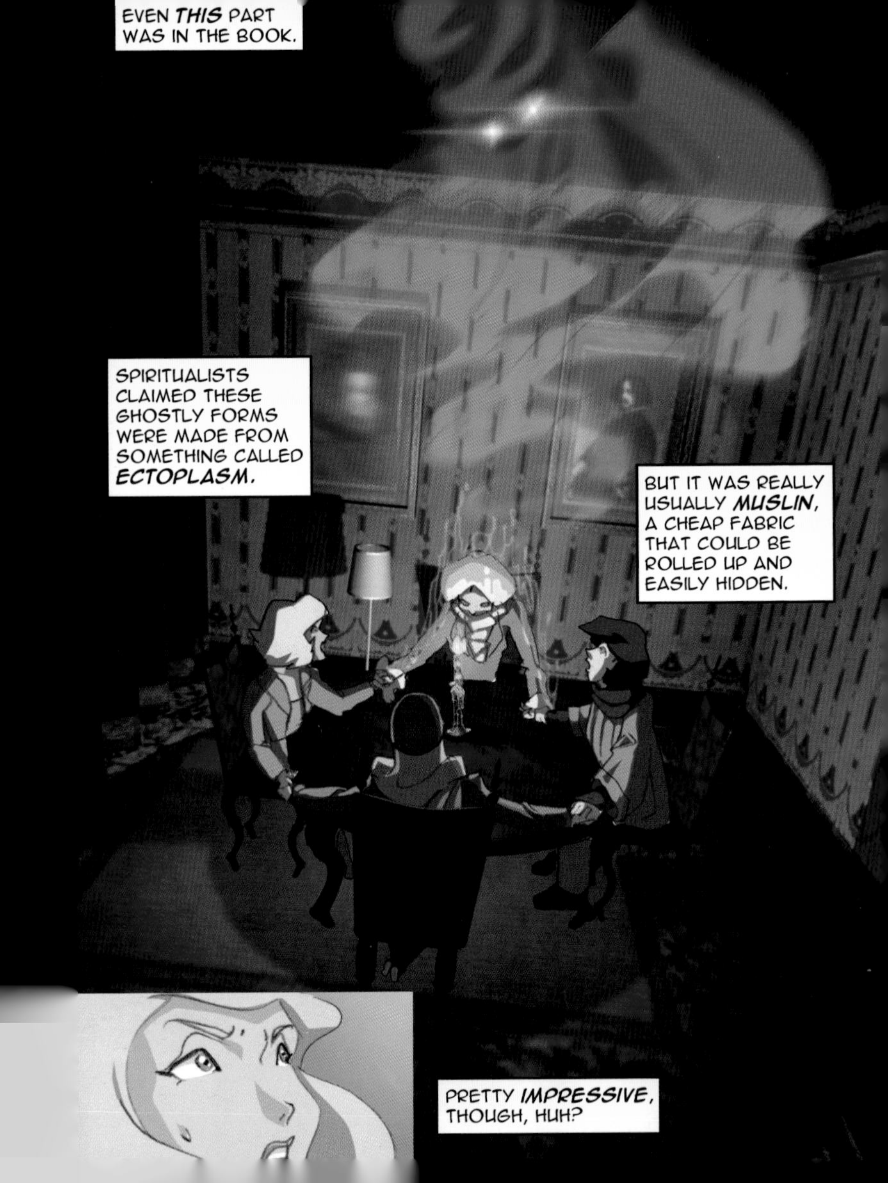
EVEN *THIS* PART WAS IN THE BOOK.
SPIRITUALISTS CLAIMED THESE GHOSTLY FORMS WERE MADE FROM SOMETHING CALLED *ECTOPLASM*.
BUT IT WAS REALLY USUALLY *MUSLIN*, A CHEAP FABRIC THAT COULD BE ROLLED UP AND EASILY HIDDEN.
PRETTY *IMPRESSIVE*, THOUGH, HUH?

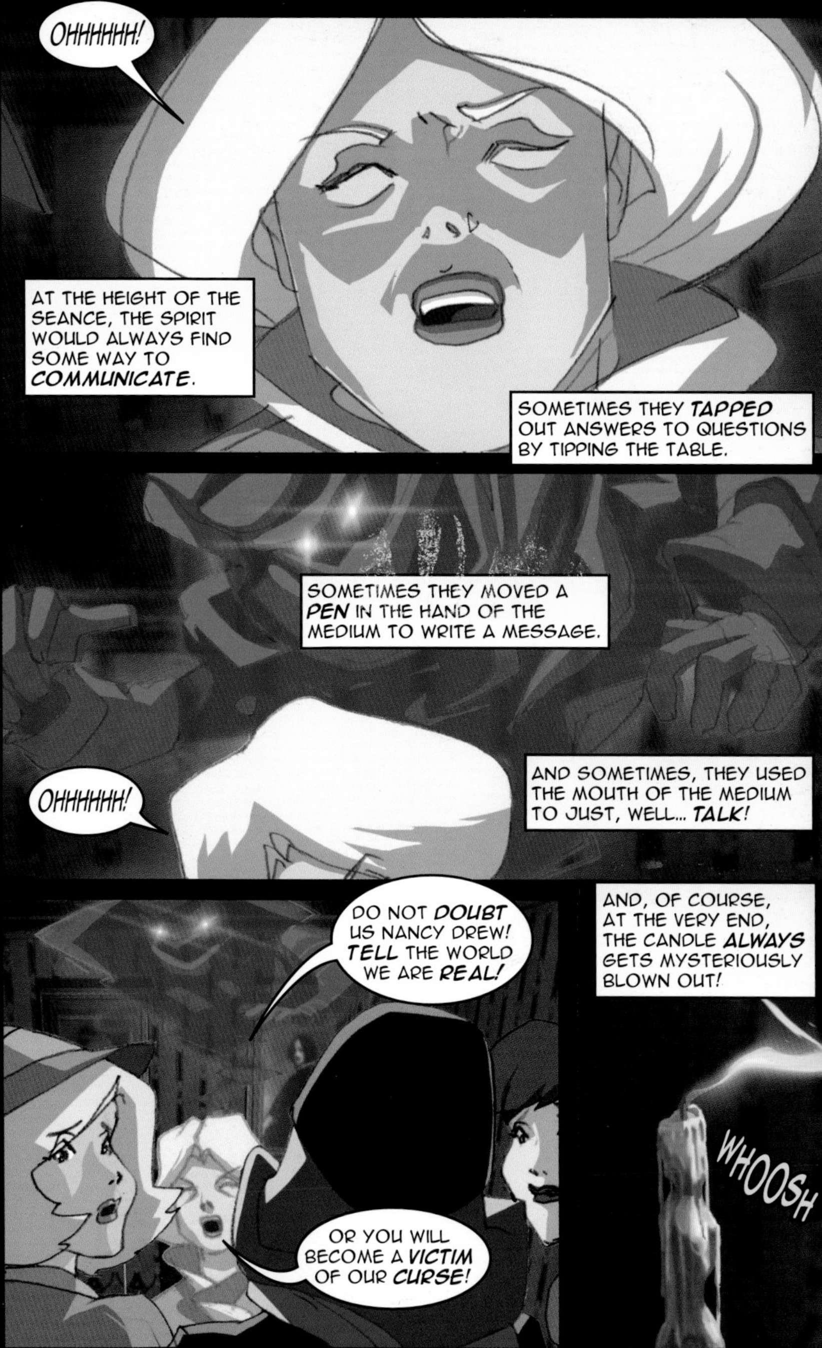
OHHHHHH!
AT THE HEIGHT OF THE SEANCE, THE SPIRIT WOULD ALWAYS FIND SOME WAY TO COMMUNICATE.
SOMETIMES THEY TAPPED OUT ANSWERS TO QUESTIONS BY TIPPING THE TABLE.
SOMETIMES THEY MOVED A PEN IN THE HAND OF THE MEDIUM TO WRITE A MESSAGE.
OHHHHHH!
AND SOMETIMES, THEY USED THE MOUTH OF THE MEDIUM TO JUST, WELL... TALK!
DO NOT DOUBT US NANCY DREW! TELL THE WORLD WE ARE REAL!
OR YOU WILL BECOME A VICTIM OF OUR CURSE!
AND, OF COURSE, AT THE VERY END, THE CANDLE ALWAYS GETS MYSTERIOUSLY BLOWN OUT!
WHOOSH

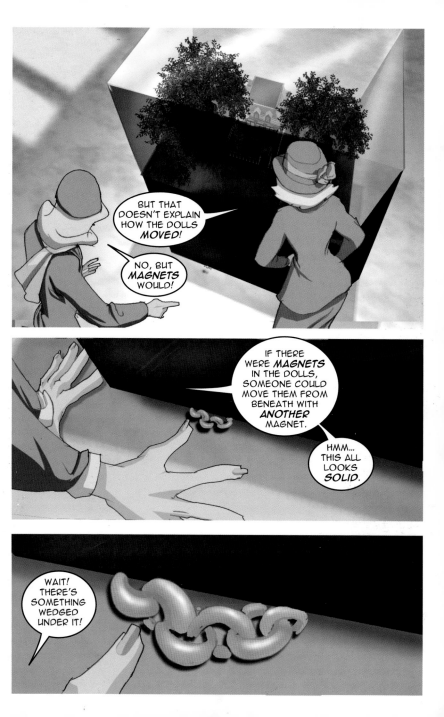

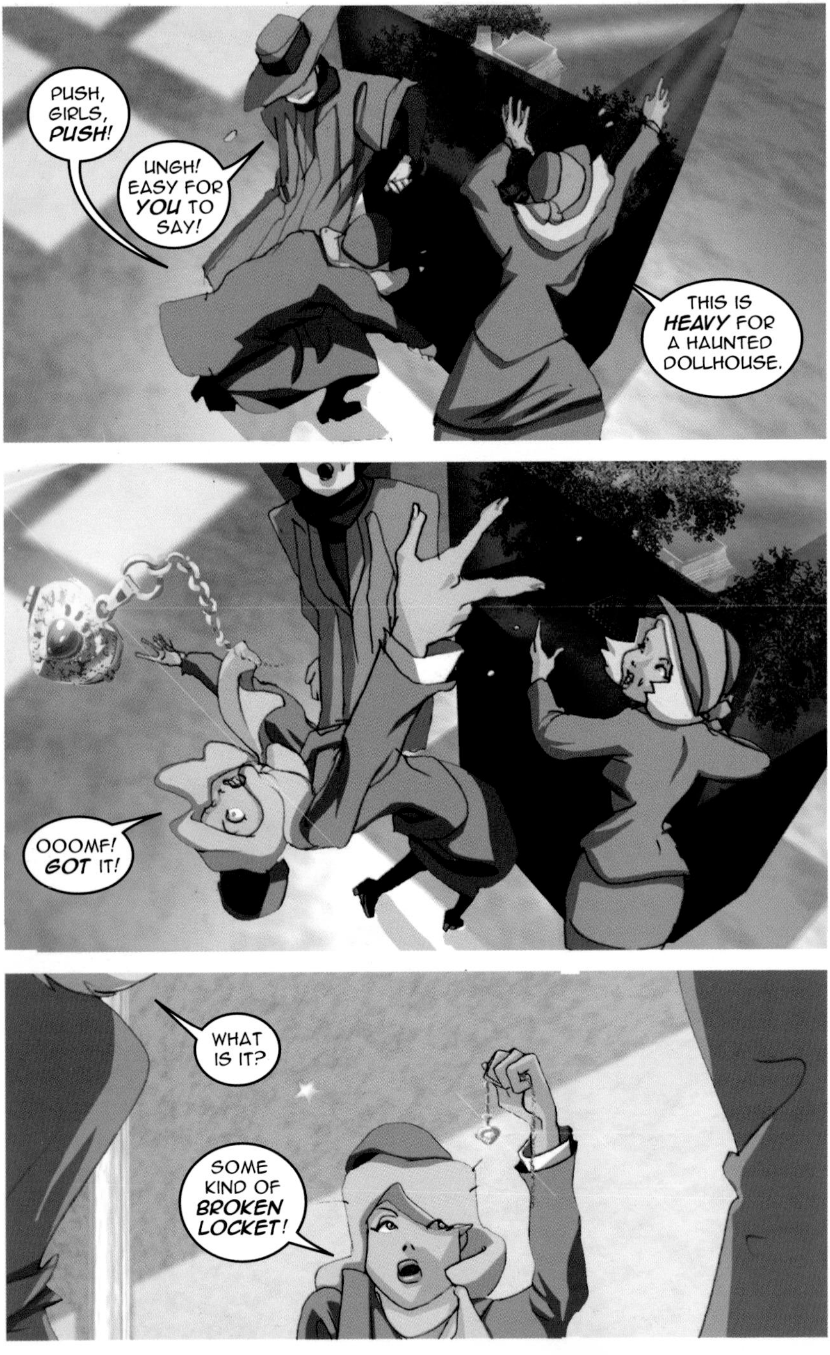
PUSH, GIRLS, **PUSH**!
UNGH! EASY FOR **YOU** TO SAY!
THIS IS **HEAVY** FOR A HAUNTED DOLLHOUSE.
OOOMF! **GOT** IT!
WHAT IS IT?
SOME KIND OF **BROKEN LOCKET**!

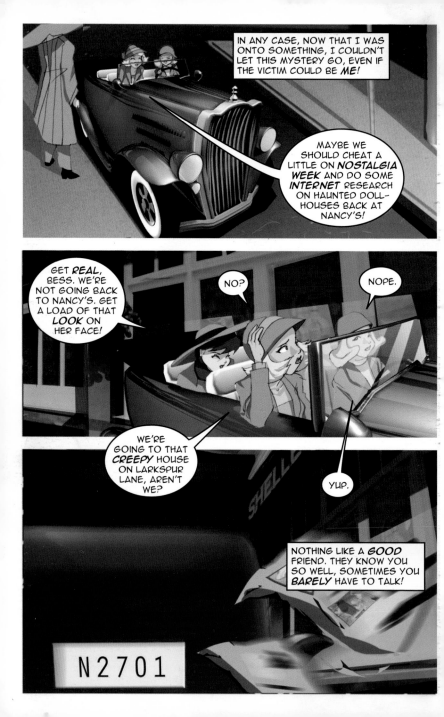

N2701

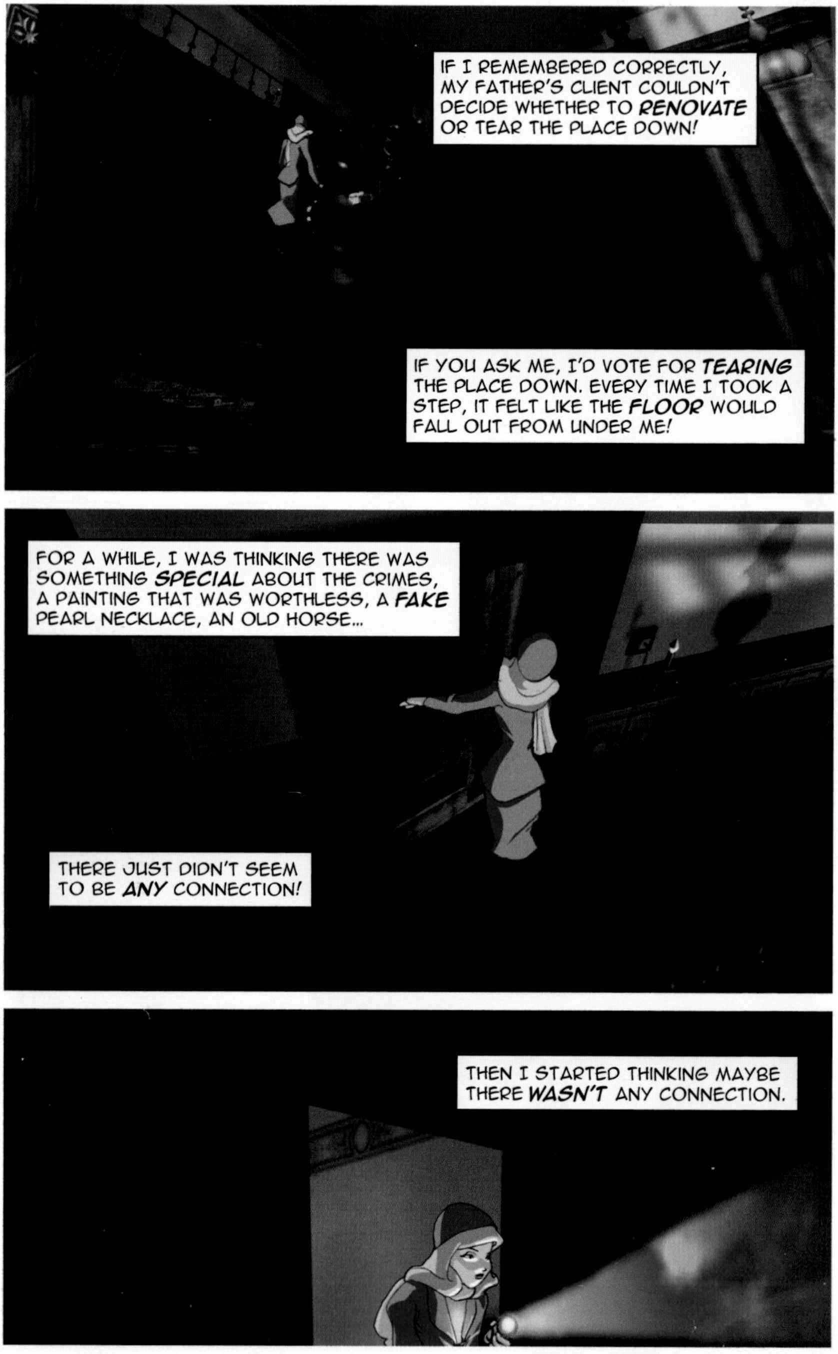
IF I REMEMBERED CORRECTLY, MY FATHER'S CLIENT COULDN'T DECIDE WHETHER TO RENOVATE OR TEAR THE PLACE DOWN!
IF YOU ASK ME, I'D VOTE FOR TEARING THE PLACE DOWN. EVERY TIME I TOOK A STEP, IT FELT LIKE THE FLOOR WOULD FALL OUT FROM UNDER ME!
FOR A WHILE, I WAS THINKING THERE WAS SOMETHING SPECIAL ABOUT THE CRIMES, A PAINTING THAT WAS WORTHLESS, A FAKE PEARL NECKLACE, AN OLD HORSE...
THERE JUST DIDN'T SEEM TO BE ANY CONNECTION!
THEN I STARTED THINKING MAYBE THERE WASN'T ANY CONNECTION.

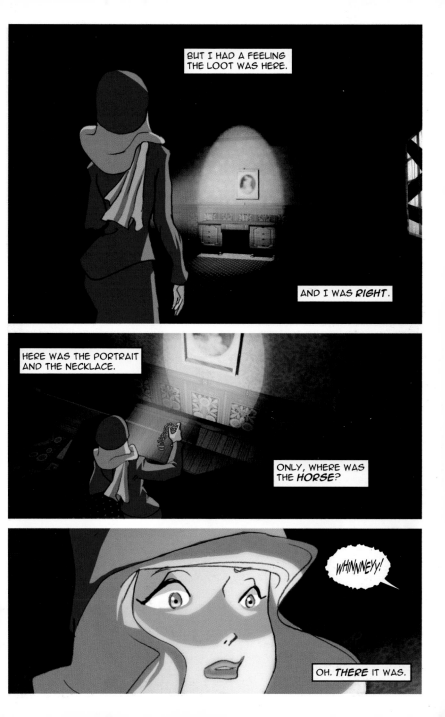

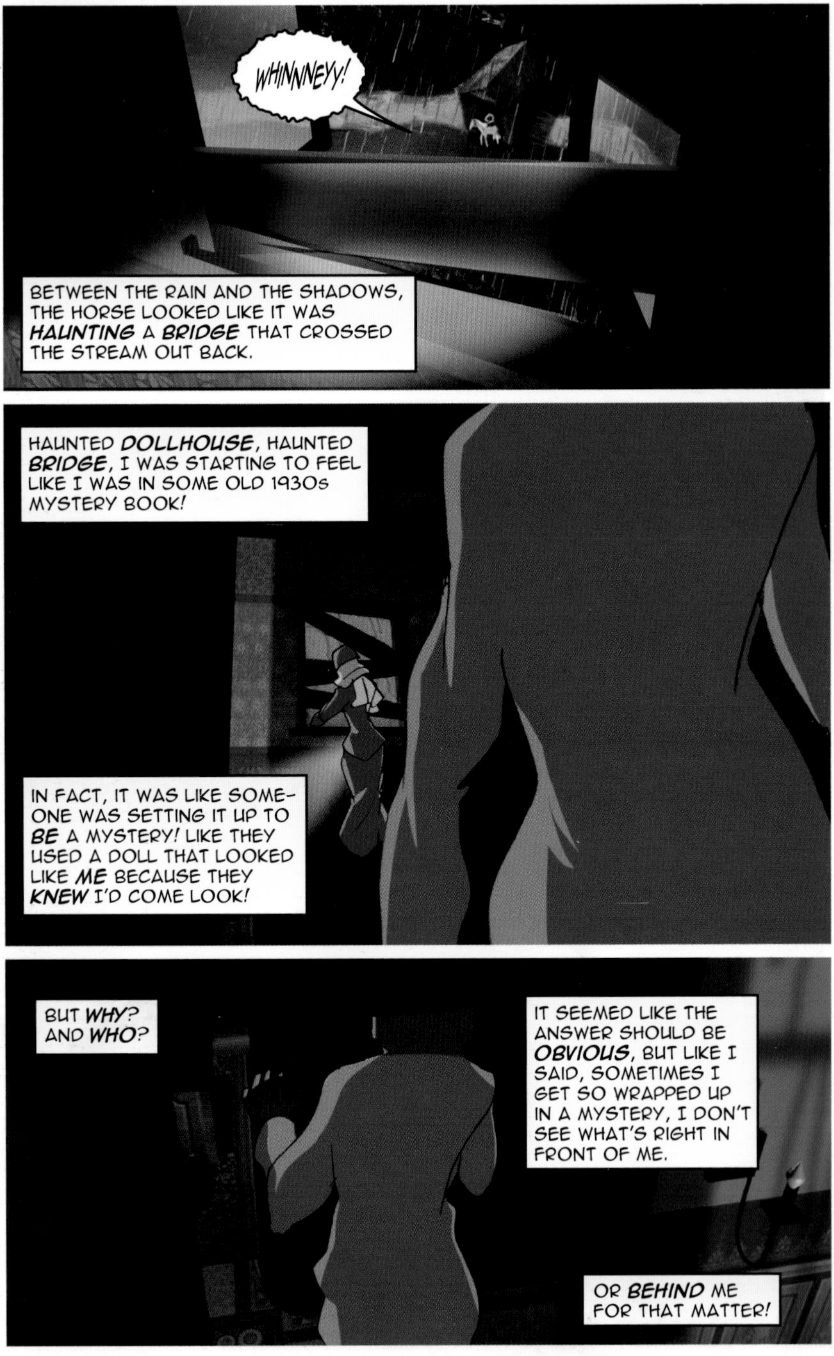

WHINNNEYY!
BETWEEN THE RAIN AND THE SHADOWS, THE HORSE LOOKED LIKE IT WAS HAUNTING A BRIDGE THAT CROSSED THE STREAM OUT BACK.
HAUNTED DOLLHOUSE, HAUNTED BRIDGE, I WAS STARTING TO FEEL LIKE I WAS IN SOME OLD 1930s MYSTERY BOOK!
IN FACT, IT WAS LIKE SOME-ONE WAS SETTING IT UP TO BE A MYSTERY! LIKE THEY USED A DOLL THAT LOOKED LIKE ME BECAUSE THEY KNEW I'D COME LOOK!
BUT WHY? AND WHO?
IT SEEMED LIKE THE ANSWER SHOULD BE OBVIOUS, BUT LIKE I SAID, SOMETIMES I GET SO WRAPPED UP IN A MYSTERY, I DON'T SEE WHAT'S RIGHT IN FRONT OF ME.
OR BEHIND ME FOR THAT MATTER!

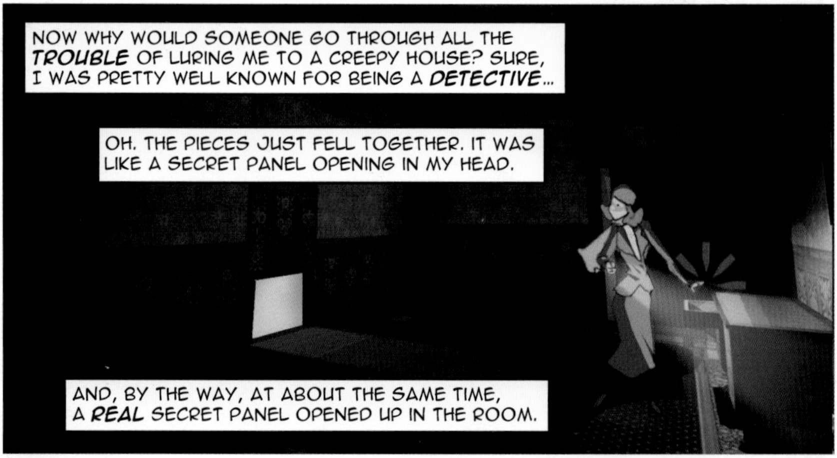
NOW WHY WOULD SOMEONE GO THROUGH ALL THE TROUBLE OF LURING ME TO A CREEPY HOUSE? SURE, I WAS PRETTY WELL KNOWN FOR BEING A DETECTIVE...
OH. THE PIECES JUST FELL TOGETHER. IT WAS LIKE A SECRET PANEL OPENING IN MY HEAD.
AND, BY THE WAY, AT ABOUT THE SAME TIME, A REAL SECRET PANEL OPENED UP IN THE ROOM.

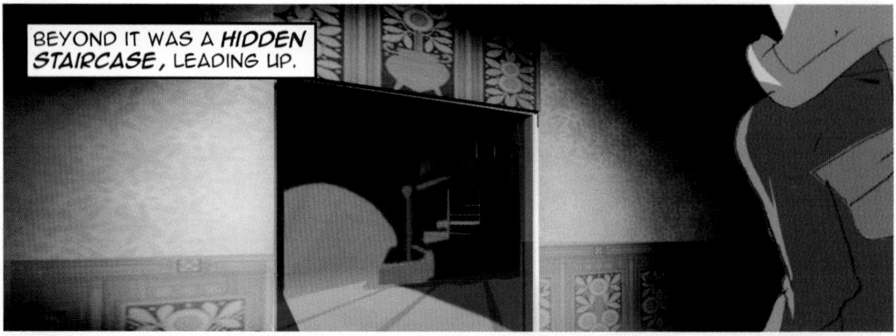
BEYOND IT WAS A HIDDEN STAIRCASE, LEADING UP.

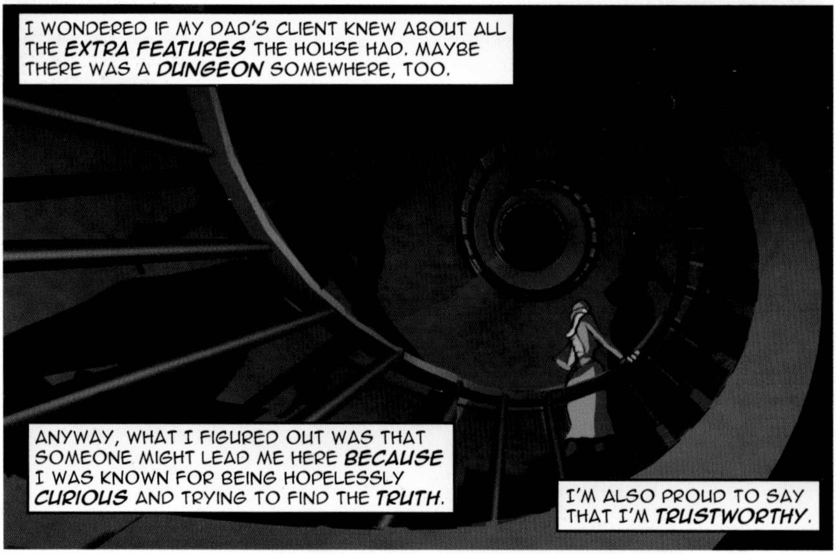
I WONDERED IF MY DAD'S CLIENT KNEW ABOUT ALL THE EXTRA FEATURES THE HOUSE HAD. MAYBE THERE WAS A DUNGEON SOMEWHERE, TOO.
ANYWAY, WHAT I FIGURED OUT WAS THAT SOMEONE MIGHT LEAD ME HERE BECAUSE I WAS KNOWN FOR BEING HOPELESSLY CURIOUS AND TRYING TO FIND THE TRUTH.
I'M ALSO PROUD TO SAY THAT I'M TRUSTWORTHY.

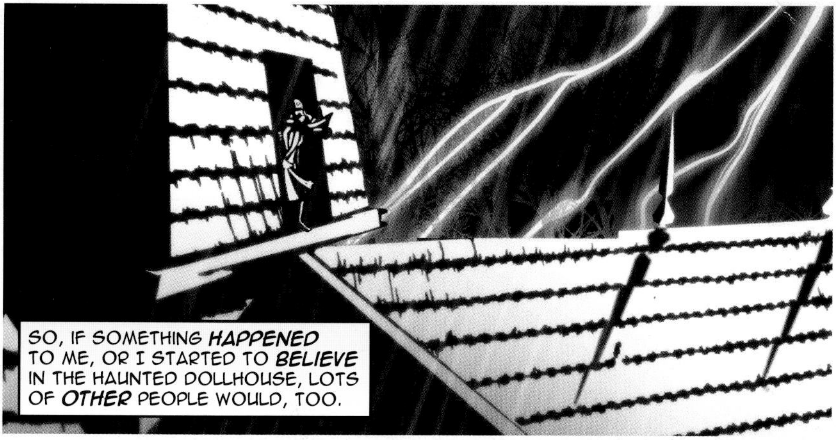
SO, IF SOMETHING HAPPENED TO ME, OR I STARTED TO BELIEVE IN THE HAUNTED DOLLHOUSE, LOTS OF OTHER PEOPLE WOULD, TOO.

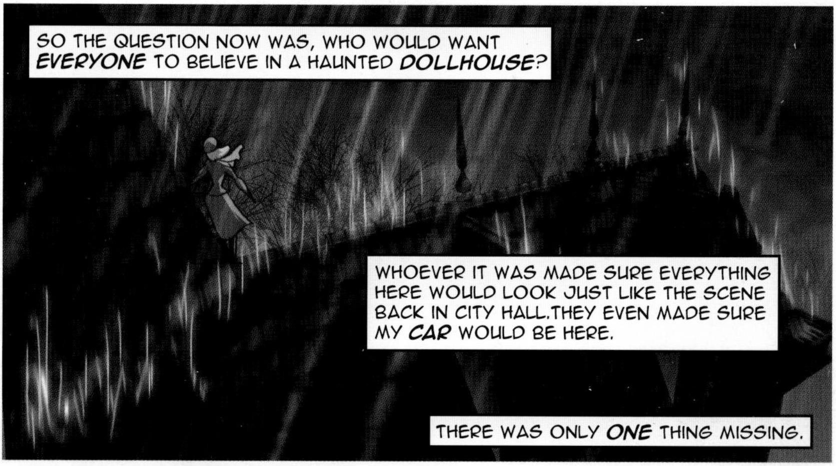
SO THE QUESTION NOW WAS, WHO WOULD WANT EVERYONE TO BELIEVE IN A HAUNTED DOLLHOUSE?
WHOEVER IT WAS MADE SURE EVERYTHING HERE WOULD LOOK JUST LIKE THE SCENE BACK IN CITY HALL.THEY EVEN MADE SURE MY CAR WOULD BE HERE.
THERE WAS ONLY ONE THING MISSING.

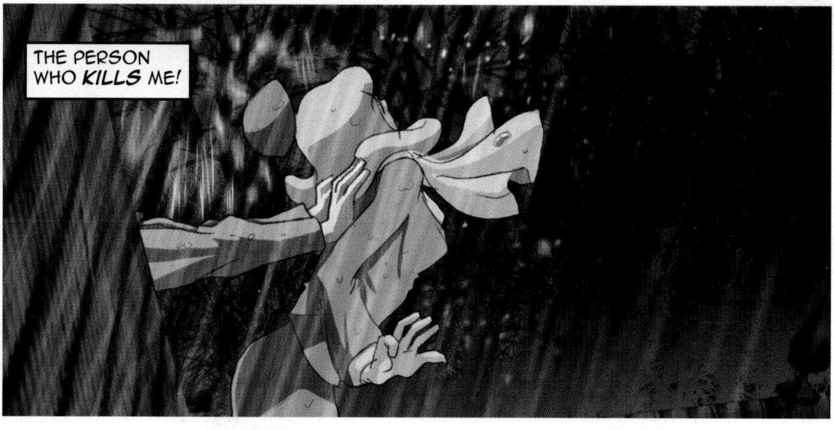
THE PERSON WHO KILLS ME!

ALL OF A SUDDEN, I DIDN'T THINK CURIOSITY WAS SUCH A GREAT CHARACTER TRAIT!
IT IS, AFTER ALL, WHAT PUTS ME IN SITUATIONS LIKE THIS IN THE FIRST PLACE.
ON THE OTHER HAND, IT'S ALSO WHAT HELPS ME FIGURE THINGS OUT!
YOU'RE NO VISITOR FROM THE SPIRIT WORLD, THAT'S FOR SURE! IN FACT, I'M PRETTY SURE YOU'RE...

NANCY DREW HERE, DEALING WITH A DIFFERENT KIND OF MYSTERY – THE MYSTERY OF MODERN TECHNOLOGY!

I THINK COMPUTERS ARE TERRIFIC – EXCEPT WHEN THEY DON'T **WORK**.

GEORGE COULD CLEAR THIS UP IN A MINUTE, BUT SHE AND BESS WERE AT A FAMILY REUNION IN OHIO AND I DIDN'T WANT TO DRAG HER AWAY FROM THE PARTY.

AGHHH!

THE GIRL WHO WASN'T THERE
CHAPTER ONE:
HERE, THERE AND EVERYWHERE!

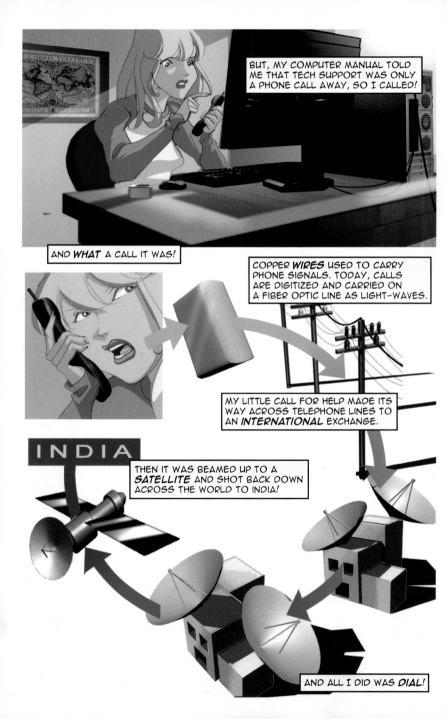

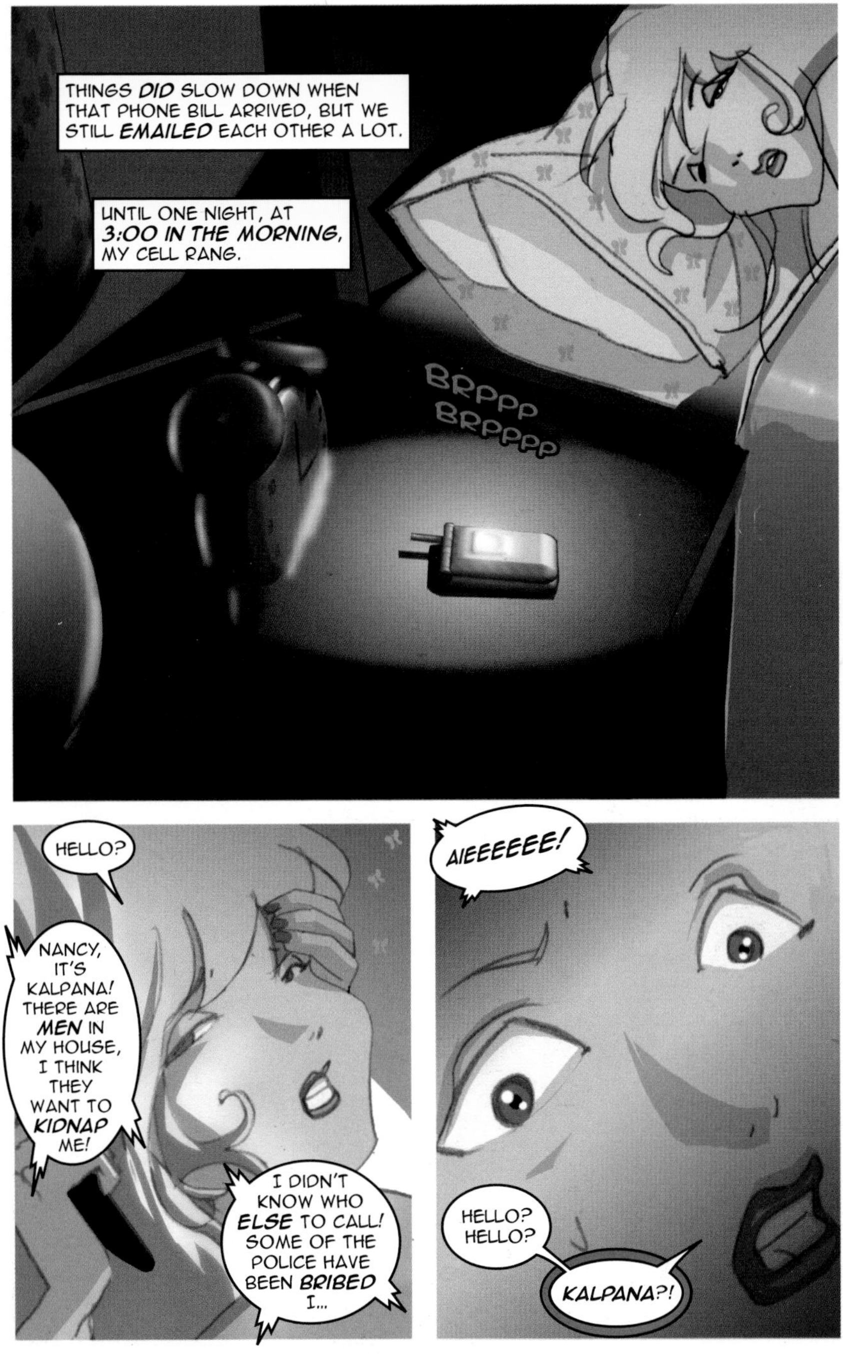
THINGS DID SLOW DOWN WHEN THAT PHONE BILL ARRIVED, BUT WE STILL EMAILED EACH OTHER A LOT.
UNTIL ONE NIGHT, AT 3:00 IN THE MORNING, MY CELL RANG.
BRPPP BRPPPP
HELLO?
NANCY, IT'S KALPANA! THERE ARE MEN IN MY HOUSE, I THINK THEY WANT TO KIDNAP ME!
I DIDN'T KNOW WHO ELSE TO CALL! SOME OF THE POLICE HAVE BEEN BRIBED I...
AIEEEEEE!
HELLO? HELLO?
KALPANA?!

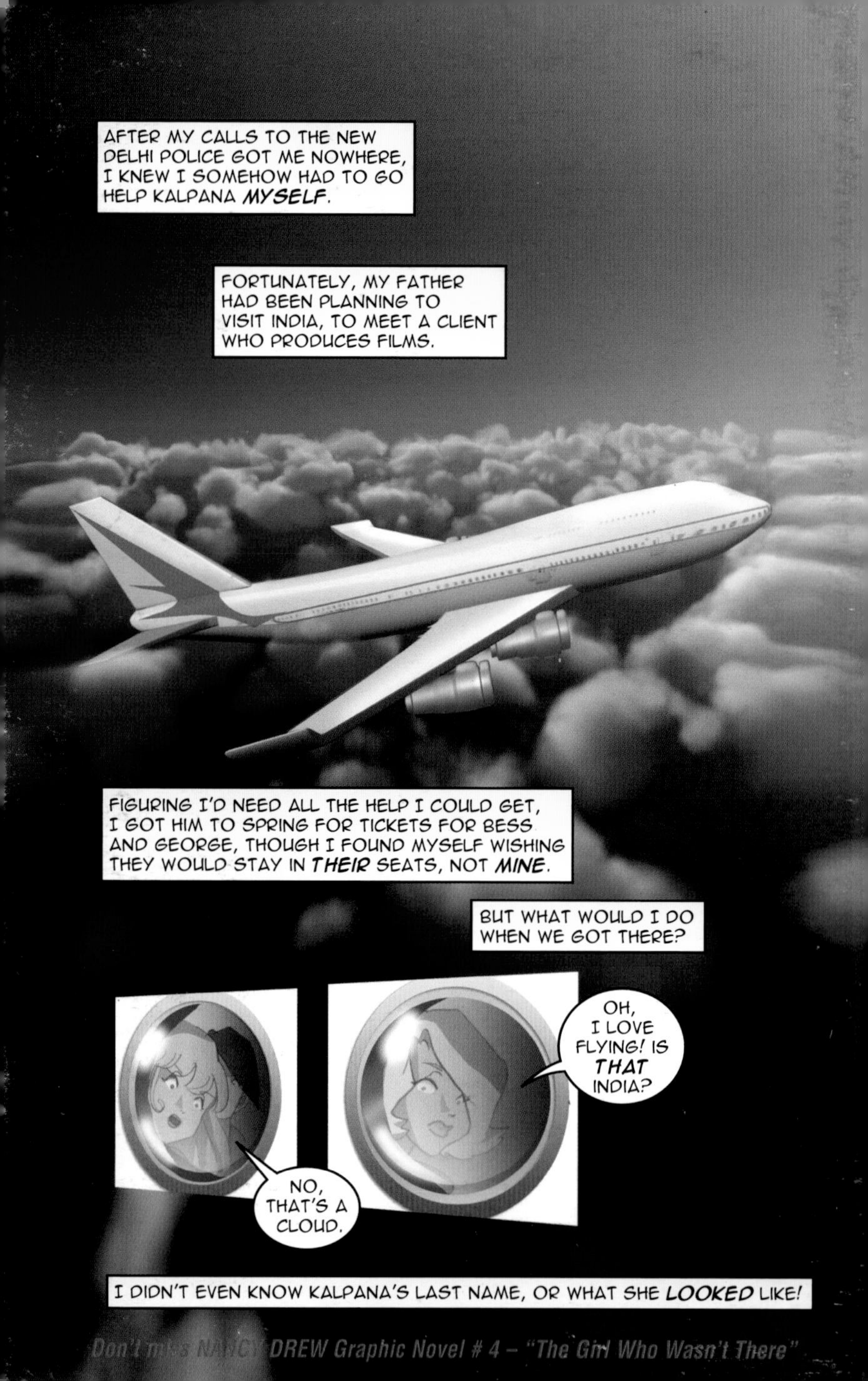
AFTER MY CALLS TO THE NEW DELHI POLICE GOT ME NOWHERE, I KNEW I SOMEHOW HAD TO GO HELP KALPANA *MYSELF*.
FORTUNATELY, MY FATHER HAD BEEN PLANNING TO VISIT INDIA, TO MEET A CLIENT WHO PRODUCES FILMS.
FIGURING I'D NEED ALL THE HELP I COULD GET, I GOT HIM TO SPRING FOR TICKETS FOR BESS AND GEORGE, THOUGH I FOUND MYSELF WISHING THEY WOULD STAY IN *THEIR* SEATS, NOT *MINE*.
BUT WHAT WOULD I DO WHEN WE GOT THERE?
OH, I LOVE FLYING! IS *THAT* INDIA?
NO, THAT'S A CLOUD.
I DIDN'T EVEN KNOW KALPANA'S LAST NAME, OR WHAT SHE *LOOKED* LIKE!